Praise for
THE BLUESUIT CHRONICLES

"*The War Comes Home* would make an excellent TV series. The book features police work from the vantagepoint of the policeman, emphasizing the exposure to the danger of police work, as you carefully work around the restraints set forth in the law. I know the public does not realize what the cop is up-against, and this book sets forth that scenario without fault. The major bestseller *The New Centurions*, by Joseph Wambaugh, is a book I will never forget, and your book is equal to his." ~Patrick Lowe, Anderson Island, WA

"The first installment of The Bluesuit Chronicles, (*The War Comes Home*) is a compelling start to what is sure to be an epic saga. A former Golden Gloves boxer and Army medic returns home from Vietnam to a very different America than the one he left. The drug craze of the early seventies takes a heavy toll on the Boomer generation, and the social fabric begins to unravel, nail-biting action, romance, and intrigue, based on actual events." Rated Four Stars.
~ Red City Reviews

"An exciting, read, riveting action, romance and moving scenes. *The War Comes Home* took me back to the Bellevue I knew in 'the good old days.' Impossible to put down." ~ Cynthia Davis, Bellevue, WA

"*The War Comes Home* follows the activities of two city police officers, Hitchcock and Walker, as they prepare and then head out for the nightly patrol of their Neighborhood streets. Hitchcock feels a strange foreboding that there will be danger that evening, and someone will die. The two police officers spend the evening patrolling areas looking for drug dealers, prostitutes, and other criminals.

This manuscript is extremely well-written. The author has infused the prose with an interesting mix of dialogue, inner thoughts. The characters are nicely developed, the dialogue is genuine and flows organically. The reader is immediately drawn into the story and wants to learn more, not only about the officers, but what awaits them as they begin their nightly patrol." ~ Editor at BookBaby

Praise For
THE BLUESUIT CHRONICLES

"Having grown up in Bellevue in the '60s and '70s, I bought the entire series for my husband for his birthday. He is completely engrossed in them. Thank you, John, for writing them, it's hard to get him to relax, and the books are doing it with laughter and 'do you remember' comments. We are eagerly waiting for the next book to come out."
~ Jeanie Hack, Bellevue, WA

"From the moment I started reading *The War Comes Home*, I couldn't put it down. I was captivated by the balance of action and drama that John Hansen expertly weaves throughout this fast-paced historical fiction. I'm looking forward to reading the next one."
~ S. McDonald, Redmond, WA

"Book 2 of The Bluesuit Chronicles series, *The New Darkness*, continues the story of Vietnam veteran Roger Hitchcock, now a police officer in Bellevue, Washington. The spreading new drug culture is taking a heavy toll on Hitchcock's generation. Some die, some are permanently impaired, everyone is impacted by this wave of evil that even turns traditional values inside out. Like other officer, the times test Hitchcock: will he resign in disgust, become hardened and bitter, corrupt, or will his background in competition boxing and military combat experience enable him to rise to meet the challenge? Romance, intrigue and action are the fabric of *The New Darkness*."
~ Amazon Review

"*Valley of Long Shadows* is the third book in The Bluesuit Chronicles... Returning Vietnam veterans who become police officers find themselves holding the line against societal anarchy. Even traditional roles between cops and robbers in police work have become more deadly...The backdrop is one of government betrayal, societal breakdown, and an angry disillusioned public. The '70s is the decade that brought America where it is now.
Four Stars Rating ~ Red City Reviews

Praise For
THE BLUESUIT CHRONICLES

"By the time I finished reading the series up through Book 4 (*Day Shift*), I concluded most men would like to be Hitchcock, at least in some way. What sets him apart is the dichotomy of his makeup: he grew up with a Boy Scout sense of honor and right and wrong, yet he isn't hardened or jaded by the evil and cruelty he saw when he went to war, though he killed in combat. As a policeman he *chooses* good and right: to do otherwise is unthinkable. He is a skilled fighter, yet so modest that he doesn't know he is a role model for others around him, and women feel safe with him. I know Hitchcock's type—two of my relatives were cops who influenced my life:"
~ Tracy Smith, Newcastle, WA

"Book 5 (*Unfinished Business*) moves to show how difficult it is for Officer Hitchcock to do right. Bad people are out to get him for his good work. He is a threat to their nefarious activities. There is even a very bad high-ranking policeman who puts Hitchcock and his family in extreme peril. Organized foreign crime is moving into his city, he works hard to uncover the clues to solve this evil in his city. I'm still waiting to find out what restaurant owner Juju is up to and who she works for. Great series and story. Another fine book by John Hansen. Yo! ~ T.A. Smith

"I've read all of John's books and rated them all 5 stars, because those stars are earned. I worked the street with John as a police officer for years and what he speaks of in his books is real. John is an excellent author; articulate and clear, always bringing the reader directly into the story. I like John's work to the point that I've asked him to send me any new books he writes; I'll be either the first or almost the first to read all of them. I lived this with John. He's an author not to be missed. You can't go wrong reading his books. I strongly encourage more in the series." ~ Bill Cooper, Chief of Police (ret)

Praise For
THE BLUESUIT CHRONICLES

"John Hansen has written another great read. *Unfinished Business* is filled with conspiracy, corruption and crime, much of which is targeted at Hitchcock. From the beginning of the book, I was hooked. The author has a gift with words that drew me into the story effortlessly— I could not put the book down. I have read all in the series and I look forward to reading more of John Hansen's books." ~ S. McDonald

"A viewpoint from the inside: I worked with and partnered with John both in uniform and in detectives, and like him I came to the Department after military service. This is the fifth (as of this date) of five books in this series. I have read and re-read all five books, and for the first time, recently, over a two-day period, read the entire series in order. All five books were inspired by John's experiences, during many of which I was present. John is an extremely gifted author, and I was transported back to those times and experienced a full gamut of emotions, mostly good, sometimes less so. His use of humor, love, anger, fear, camaraderie, loyalty, respect, disapproval, devotion, and other emotions, rang true throughout the books." ~ Robert Littlejohn

"The whole series of The Bluesuit Chronicles brought back a flood of memories. I started in police work in 1976. This series starts a couple of years earlier. The descriptions of the equipment, the way you had to solve crimes without the assistance of modern items. John made me feel that I was there when it was happening. This whole series is what police work is about. Working with citizens, caring about them, and catching the bad guys. Officers in that time period cared about what they did. It wasn't all about a paycheck... We were the originators of community policing. We knew our beat and the people in it. I am not saying we were perfect; however, we were very committed to our community. That being said, I can't wait for the next book. Please read the whole series. Once you start you won't stop."
~ Garry C. Dixon, Ret. LEO-Virginia

Praise For
THE BLUESUIT CHRONICLES

"Received Book 4, *Day Shift*, on a Wednesday. Already done reading it. Couldn't help myself. Was only going to read a couple chapters and save the rest for my upcoming camping trip. LOL. 3 hours later book finished. Love it. 2 Thumbs up!!! ~ Alanda Bailey, Kalispell, MT

"Retired Detective John Hansen is a master writer. He brings to life policing in the Northwestern U.S. during the '70s, a transitional period. One has to wonder of how much of his writings are founded in personal experience vs. creative thinking. Either way, his stories are thoroughly enjoyable and well-worth purchasing his original books in this series, his current release, as well as the books yet to come."
~ Debbie M.-Scottsdale, AZ

"I urge you to complete your 'to do' list prior to reading *Unfinished Business*, as once started, I could not put it down. It was always, 'one more page' and soon I was not getting anything else done, but it was well worth it. The author has an amazing way of drawing the reader into each scene, adding to the excitement, sweet romance, raw emotion and revealing of each fascinating character as the plots unfold. I highly recommend this book to anyone who wants a truly good read. Looking forward to the next book from this highly talented author." ~ Cynthia R.

"I received Book 5 in The Bluesuit Chronicles and started reading and per usual, didn't stop until I finished the book. I am a huge fan of John's stories. I grew up in the general area that the stories are set in. Also, in the same timeframe. John's books are always fast paced and entertaining reads. I would recommend them to any and all."
~ A. Bailey-Kalispell, MT

Also by John Hansen:

The Award -Winning Series: The Bluesuit Chronicles:

Published & Award -Winning Essays and Short Stories:

Non-Fiction Book:

Day Shift

Book 4 of The Bluesuit Chronicles

JOHN HANSEN

Day Shift
by John Hansen

This book is a work of fiction. Names, characters, locations and events are either a product of the author's imagination, fictitious or used fictitiously. Any resemblance to any event, locale or person, living or dead, is purely coincidental.

Third Edition
Revised and Reprinted - Copyright © 2020 John Hansen
Original Copyright © 2017 John Hansen

Cover Designer: Jessica Bell - Jessica Bell Design
Interior Design and Formatting: Deborah J Ledford - IOF Productions Ltd

Issued in Print and Electronic Formats
Trade Paperback ISBN: 978-1735803036

Manufactured in the United States of America

Day Shift

JOHN HANSEN

To Patricia, my loving bride, you are my Ruth,
I am your Boaz.

The Bluesuit Chronicles series is dedicated to the men and women who answered the call to serve and protect, whether in a military or law enforcement capacity, so others can sleep at night.

Chace's Pancake Corral is the most frequent setting in the series. It is one of the last icons of Old Bellevue, Washington, of which it is said, "If you say you live in Bellevue and don't know about the Pancake Corral, you're either new in town or a liar!" *Day Shift* is dedicated to the Pancake Corral and to the memory of its founders, Bill and Louise Chace.

*"In those days Israel had no king.
Everyone did as he saw fit."*

~ Judges 17:6

AUTHOR'S NOTE

Don't expect tidy plots, or The Bluesuit Chronicles to be traditional novels that follow the tired old rebellion-ruin-restoration arc. The stories are unpredictable because they are based on actual events of the '70s, a period of weak leadership and perilous decline that foreshadowed the 21st Century.

Police officers and detectives can't solve every crime. Despite their best efforts, criminals sometimes skate because of a legal technicality, a smart defense attorney, a weak prosecutor, judge, or jury. Cops often become cynical as they face unending conflict on the streets, within their departments, within city hall, within the community. Not every issue is resolved. Not every hidden agenda is exposed. That's life.

Rather than tidy predictability found in traditional novels, here you'll experience gritty authenticity, cop humor, camaraderie, action, romance, intrigue and unexpected twists—based on actual events.

~John Hansen

ABOUT THE NEW COVER

Cover designer Jessica Bell and I went the extra mile in redoing the cover of *Day Shift*. Great care was taken to present on the front and back covers a patrol car of the correct make and model, having the correct markings, equipment. We did this by locating old original black-and-white photographs and searching the internet. The cruisers shown are 1971 Plymouth Fury sedans with two white doors (as opposed to four, which came later) and a white roof, as it was in those days.

PROLOGUE

New Year's Day 1971 - Friday, 3:49 A.M.
Police Station
Bellevue, Washington

IN THE COLD pre-dawn fog, a grayish green '59 Volvo pv544 sedan, a tank-like car, engine and headlights off, coasted like a ghost ship down the gentle slope of the Bellevue City Hall parking lot. The driver felt his stomach churning as he let out the clutch and braked to a stop at the spot he selected earlier for this very time. He was a few yards above the police parking lot. His hands were cold and clammy. Any minute now, off-duty officers would be coming out of the station.

He counted nine black-and-white cruisers in the parking lot as he waited. *The night shift officers are still all in the station, the morning shift hasn't left yet, so the city is unprotected every day at this time—good to know.*

From previous visits he learned the shift schedules of the Patrol Division and where officers come in and

1

out of the station on the bottom floor of the three-story City Hall.

His nerves tingled as he waited for a certain officer to emerge. whose photograph he had on the seat next to him. His binoculars were in his lap, a magnum revolver rested inside his back waistband. It certainly was cold sitting there, motionless. From time to time he rubbed his hands on his thighs and tucked them into his armpits for warmth. He put his binoculars on each officer that came out but none were the one in the photograph.

He hadn't mentioned a word of this to his comrades for a reason. Not that they wouldn't approve—they would, but for ideological reasons. Not him. His beef with this cop was a personal business matter. He worried that his former cellmates would stupidly claim responsibility for his act to gain publicity for their cause. The law dogs would pounce on them if they did. His parole would be over, a lucrative source of personal income would be lost, and their fledgling brigade would be crushed before they rallied the people and ignited the revolution.

He wished his comrades to be content to resume making bombs after they sobered up.

HE WATCHED EIGHT OFFICERS make their way to their cruisers, checked their equipment and leave. The morning shift was on duty but the personal cars of the night shift officers hadn't moved. They were still in the station. He waited.

Almost two hours later, off-duty officers wearing civilian jackets over their dark blue uniforms trickled out of the station. They passed in front of him, unaware of his presence, headed for their personal vehicles. *Must have been busy last night to be getting off this late*, he concluded as he studied each officer with binoculars.

After sitting in numbing cold this long without a glimpse of his intended victim, he concluded the officer he was after took the night off, it being New Year's Eve.

He thought he knew where to find him.

Instead of returning to Seattle, he drove west on the Main Street overpass of the 405 freeway, heading uphill toward Bellevue's downtown.

The city slept, the streets were empty and it was getting light.

CHAPTER ONE
A Mexican Standoff

New Year's Day 1971 - Friday, 6:00 A.M.
Bellevue, Washington
Police Station

HITCHCOCK SQUINTED AS he stepped of the station into the bright sunlight. It was cold. He flipped up the collar and shoved his hands into the pockets of his gray wool Filson hunting jacket.

The empty streets seemed exhausted as he drove out of the station parking lot. It was the first day of a three-day weekend and much of the city was sleeping off another raucous New Year's Eve.

The night before had been a wild last hurrah for Sergeant Jack Breen's squad before it rotated to mornings. Nine hours of non-stop disturbance calls to bars, parking lot fights, loud parties, underage keggers in the woods, and of course the usual nailing of drunk drivers. Even with officers called in on overtime to beef

5

up the squad, no one had time to eat.

Hitchcock came in on his night off. He stayed two hours past end of shift to help married officers with reports and prisoner bookings so they could go home to their families.

Tuning his AM radio to KJR, the throbbing beat of Norman Greenbaum's hit song, *Spirit in the Sky* boosted his energy for the short drive home. He turned right on Main Street from the station.

From out of the blue came the knowledge that Allie was in danger. He flipped a U-turn and sped across the Main Street overpass of I-405 toward her apartment.

He sped into the first intersection at 112th Avenue without looking. A long horn blast and the sound of skidding tires came from his left. A station wagon was about to hit him broadside.

He stomped on the gas and swerved right, escaping collision by inches. He stopped at the curb on the other side of the intersection, panting, facing uphill, his heart pounding.

The driver of the station wagon got out, his face purple with rage, shouting as he pointed at the traffic signal above. In his rush to get to Allie, he entered an intersection against a red light.

His heart continued pounding as he gripped the steering wheel with both hands, his foot on the brake pedal. He had barely missed being killed.

The other driver stood at his door, shaking his finger, yelling unintelligibly.

He shook his head and lifted his hands, palms up. "Sorry sir. No harm, no foul, sir! I've got an emergency!" He sped uphill to the next traffic signal at 108th Avenue, just over the crest.

He stopped at the next red signal, checked in all directions, then drove against it to the next red light at 106th Avenue. Clear. The next one at 104th Avenue, the main drag, was also red. He drove through it, still on Main Street, turned right on 100th Avenue, then left, entering the Bay View Apartments parking lot, where he came upon a strange sight.

A man was breaking into the driver's door of Allie's gray Toyota with a twisted wire coat hanger. A startled look of recognition crossed his face when he turned and saw Hitchcock.

He hustled to a battered gray Volvo parked next to Allie's car, facing out.

Hitchcock recognized him from his prison mugshot as Bruce Sands, the one who had been stalking Allie under the alias of Jim Reynolds.

He blocked the Volvo in with his El Camino, got out, shed his jacket and aimed his service revolver at Sands. "Police officer! You're under arrest! Both hands on the dash, palms up and keep 'em there!"

Sands stared openmouthed at Hitchcock.

He yelled to the young man in a bus driver uniform stepping out of a ground-floor apartment, lunch-pail in hand, "Call police emergency. Tell 'em an off-duty officer is in an armed confrontation in the Bay Vue

Apartments parking lot. Tell 'em Code Three!"

"Yes, sir," he yelled and dashed back inside his apartment.

He remembered Allie told him that as Jim Reynolds, Sands showed her his gun, saying he intended to use it in a war of some kind. *Hopefully Sands doesn't know that Department-issue .38 Special ammunition couldn't penetrate windshield glass.*

Sands leaned forward, gripping the steering wheel with his left hand while his right hand disappeared behind him.

He's going for his gun, here we go. Hitchcock cocked the hammer of his service revolver.

A police siren shattered the silence. A black-and-white patrol car burst into view and stopped behind Hitchcock. Ray Packard bailed out, shotgun in hand. He jacked a round into the chamber and aimed it at Sands.

"He's got a gun, Ray!"

"Police! You're under arrest! Both hands on the dash. Palms up—Now!" Packard shouted.

Sands placed both hands on the dash in slow motion, never taking his eyes off the shotgun.

Packard nodded for Hitchcock to proceed.

The driver's door creaked when Hitchcock opened it, aiming his revolver at Sands's head.

CHAPTER TWO
The Shakedown

SANDS KEPT STARING at the shotgun. "Hands behind your head, interlock your fingers," Hitchcock ordered in a calm voice. He took hold of his fingers. "Step out slow and easy," he commanded as he holstered his gun. "Face the car, feet shoulder width apart." He went first for the gun he knew was there—a blued Charter Arms .357 Magnum revolver tucked in the back of Sands's waistband.

"Got a concealed weapon permit?" Hitchcock asked over the clicking of handcuffs.

No answer.

"What are you doing here?"

Silence.

He pulled a wallet out of Sands's hip pocket.

"You have a driver's license, Sands, but not a permit to carry a concealed weapon. Did you leave it at home?"

No reply.

"Besides being under arrest for car prowling, you're

also under arrest for unlawful carrying of a concealed weapon."

Sands said nothing.

"If you're a convicted felon in possession of a gun, that's an automatic five years tacked on to any other time you'll serve. Are you on parole or probation?"

No response.

Packard secured the shotgun. He advised Sands of his Constitutional rights and warnings.

"Watch your head getting in," Hitchcock cautioned as he guided Sands into the back seat of the patrol car. He unloaded six rounds of hollow-point ammunition from the .357 and sniffed the barrel. "Hmmm. Been shooting lately?"

Sands said nothing.

Hitchcock sealed the gun and the ammunition in separate envelopes and secured them in the trunk of the patrol car. Packard motioned with his head. They stepped out of hearing range of Sands.

"What happened?" Packard asked.

"I came here after I left the station and caught him in the act of breaking into my girlfriend's car. I recognized him from his prison mugshot. He's been dogging her for weeks under the alias of Jim Reynolds."

Packard's eyes narrowed. "An alias! What's up with that?"

"I'm still trying to figure it out."

"Let's inventory his car before the impound truck gets here," Packard said. He wheezed when he opened the driver's door of the Volvo. "Whuh! How many people died in here?"

"He had magnum hollow-points in the gun, cop-killer loads, Ray. The empty box of .38 ammo on the floor and a sniff of its barrel says he's been shooting in the last day or two."

Packard nodded knowingly. "Practicing for either a robbery or a gunfight with us, no doubt about it."

Hitchcock leaned into the backseat area of the Volvo. "Got a fast-food graveyard in here," he quipped, looking at the piles of crumpled coffee cups, greasy hamburger wrappers from McDonald's and Dick's Drive-In, empty packs of Camel cigarettes, stacks of underground prison newsletters filled with anti-American rhetoric, espousing Marxist hate, and a copy of *The Anarchist's Cookbook* covered the rear seat and floor.

"The *nerve* of guys like him calling *us* pigs!" Packard said, shaking his head. "He's not only a burglar and a car prowler, he's a radical too. Look at all this commie crap, hate propaganda for inmates."

An olive green canvas satchel on the front passenger floor caught Hitchcock's eye. It was filled to the brim with tools. Screwdrivers, pliers, pry-bars, lock picks, a slim-jim for slipping car door locks, black electricians' tape, a flashlight, thin cotton gloves.

Hitchcock held up a pry-bar, gloves and lock picks. "Do ya think we got enough to charge our upstanding citizen here with possession of burglar tools, Ray?"

"Fits the duck principle enough to suit me," Packard said.

"Duck principle?"

"If it looks like a duck, walks like a duck..."

"Aww, maybe we've misjudged the poor guy, Ray. Maybe he's a freelance mechanic down on his luck, looking for work."

Packard snapped his fingers. "I've got it! He's a freelance *locksmith* down on his luck. He came here to demonstrate his skills to potential customers, and left his concealed weapons permit at home when he switched to his *other* wallet."

"You mean his *dress* wallet, of course," Hitchcock corrected.

"Of course. And his car smells bad because he *passes gas* when he eats beans."

"No, sir. This gentleman *breaks wind* when *legumes* are his diet."

"You catch on fast, friend," Packard chuckled.

"Looks like he collected everything the statute mentions as a burglar tool, put 'em in a bag and came here, hoping we'd catch him."

"It's his off-hand way of showing us he can read," Packard said.

"He's a recent graduate of Graybar University, you know."

Packard grinned and nodded his head. "*Magna cum laude*, I'll bet. Even if he's clear of warrants, this ole boy's going downtown."

"Clear of warrants, he ain't, Ray,"

"You checked?"

"Quack," went Hitchcock, his comic side coming out.

"Quack-quack, quack-quack-quack," went Packard, the Department's stand-up comedian, hands on his chest, flapping his elbows like wings, laughing. Hitchcock did the same.

Packard returned to his cruiser. His radio crackled. Records interrupted the comedy: *"Stand by for confirmed warrant information."*

"Uh-oh, Sands, any last words before you walk the plank?"

Sands stared straight ahead, stoic, greasy hair hanging in his eyes, hands cuffed behind him.

Packard keyed his mic: "Quaaaack! One Zero One, ready to copy, Records, quack!"

The Records clerk giggled as she replied, *"The following are confirmed warrants. Two Failure to Appear warrants out of Seattle Municipal Court: One for Speeding, fifty-two in a twenty-five zone, one hundred dollars bail. Negligent Driving, one hundred fifty dollars bail."*

"Copied, quack," Packard replied. He looked over his shoulder through the steel mesh screen at Sands.

"You a betting man, Bruce?" Packard held up a five-dollar bill. "This five-spot says your gun is hot. Whattaya say?"

Sands shook his head slightly and looked away.

"No? Guess I better check, after all."

A couple minutes later: *"Records to One Zero One: Confirmed hit on a Charter Arms brand .357 Magnum, serial number 459178. Reported stolen to Seattle PD on 3-10-70."*

"Received," Packard acknowledged, shaking his head in mock dismay.

"Goll-eee, Mr. Sands! By mistake, I called it *your* gun when in fact it's *not* your gun—it's stolen! Darn smart of you not to bet."

Sands grunted and shook his dirty hair back out of his eyes as he stared out the window. His thin mustache and granny glasses gave him the evil persona of a villain in a vintage black-and-white Russian film.

Hitchcock found a small red address book under the front seat armrest. He handed it to Packard, then opened the back door of the patrol car. He winced at Sands's body odor as he leaned in.

"Hey Sands, I wonder if you'd help us out," Hitchcock asked. "We see you're from Seattle, yet you're here in an out-of-the-way place in Bellevue, at an early hour, on a holiday, packing iron. Do you know whose car you were breaking into? Any idea?"

Sands said nothing.

Another patrol unit arrived to handle the impound. Packard left for the station with Sands.

Hitchcock headed up the outside stairs for Allie's apartment.

CHAPTER THREE
Checking On Allie

ALLIE OPENED HER door. She had that fresh-out-of-bed, no makeup, mussed honey-blonde hair look that turn men into putty. Hitchcock's knees weakened. No white terrycloth bathrobe could hide a figure like hers.

"Roger! What's going on?"

When he closed his eyes, savoring her presence, he saw himself on a tropical beach with Allie in a bikini. He took her by the hand as they walked the white sand beach toward the blue-green surf...then he felt a small hand on his chest.

"Uh, Roger? Are you there?"

"Oh–yeah–I...uh, sorry, I spaced out," he said, placing his hand on hers, with a sheepish grin on his face.

"Tell me what happened!" she demanded, pulling her hand back.

He felt his face flush. "Uh–what happened–uh, sure," he said, embarrassed, collecting his thoughts.

"Happy New Year, baby."

"Come on!" she demanded. "I'm scared and you're joking around."

"Sorry. Uh, I worked late this morning—came here from the station in time to catch Sands, or 'Jim Reynolds' as you know him, breaking into your car. I arrested him and detained him until a backup arrived. I took a loaded gun off him."

"I saw that. Why the gun?" she asked, her eyes wide with fear. "This is at least the second time he's been here. I'm scared. *How* does he know where I live?"

"Obviously he's got inside information about you," Hitchcock replied. "As a felon on parole, having a gun on him has cost him his freedom. I'm going to the station to give him a chance to talk. He probably won't, but he might want to take down others who are in on this with him. Might be a couple hours, but I'll be back."

THE GRAVITY OF the situation at hand hit him as he went down the outside staircase. Sands, a hardened criminal on federal parole, sought Allie out and contacted her often under the alias of Jim Reynolds. The communist propaganda materials in his car, his political rantings, and showing her his gun begged the question: what were his intentions when he went to Allie's apartment so early, armed?

Hitchcock headed to the station, determined to find out.

CHAPTER FOUR
Little Red Book

HE FOUND PACKARD filling out an arrest sheet in the booking room. "He's in a cell. Found this on him," he said, handing Hitchcock an evidence envelope.

"What the—? A photo of me?"

"I didn't ask him about it," Packard said, "thought you'd want to."

"My photo and Sherman's were in the papers after we killed Tyrone Guyon and Mae Driscoll when they ambushed us last October."

"They put you and all the rest of us at risk."

"It wasn't the Department. It was one particular lieutenant acting without authorization, against policy."

"Bostwick?"

Hitchcock nodded.

"Any discipline?"

"Captain Delstra suspended him but he was overruled by the powers-that-be upstairs."

"So there's an anti-cop element at the top. The car he

was breaking into is your girlfriend's?"

"Correct."

"Does he know the car is hers?"

"Positive," he answered as he grabbed the cell keys from the desk.

"He says he's not talking."

"Ask me if I care."

Packard showed Hitchcock the little red address book. "You and your lady friend are in it—ask him."

His mind raced as he read Allie's name and age, her son Trevor's name and age, her address and phone number, and where she worked. On another page was the contact information of private investigator Tobias Olson. Below that, OFFICER ROGER HITCHCOCK, BELLEVUE PD in capital letters. Scowling, he said, "Thanks, Ray. I'll talk to him now."

† † †

DESPITE HIS HIPPIE appearance, Sands's eyes revealed a brainwashed hate Hitchcock had seen before in captured Viet Cong guerillas. He escorted him to an interview room and read his Constitutional rights to him again.

"I understand my rights and I'm not talking," he replied in a mechanical tone of voice.

He showed Sands the photograph. "Why was this in your car?"

Sands shrugged and said nothing.

"Okay, fine," Hitchcock said after a tense pause.

"I'm curious about one other thing."

"What?"

"Did you intend to shoot me before my backup arrived?"

A tight-lipped smirk. "The shotgun," he said.

"You had a .357. The ammo would've gone through your windshield like a hot knife through butter. Why didn't you shoot?"

"The shotgun," Sands repeated, another evil smirk.

"The people in those apartments are frightened, Sands. Quite a few have little kids. It would help a lot if they at least understood what your business there was, so early on a holiday morning, packing heat."

Sands stared at the floor. "Take−me−to−jail," he said, enunciating each word.

Hitchcock held up the photograph of himself again. "Did a private investigator named Tobias Olson give you this?"

Sands lifted his head at the sound of Olson's name. Hitchcock could see him deciding how to answer the question. He looked at the floor. "I better not say," he muttered.

"I'll take that as a yes."

Sands said nothing.

Hitchcock held up the red address book. "How much is Olson paying you to contact Allison Malloy?"

Sands rubbed his palms on his knees, shaking his head. "My game is up. There's nothing in it for me if I talk."

"I'll do my best to cut you a deal with the prosecutor if you do."

He shook his head. "You can't. My parole is federal and it's gone. I'm going back."

Hitchcock returned Sands to a cell. He turned to leave when Sands spoke.

"A question, officer?"

"Sure."

"What's with you and the other officer making duck sounds and flapping your arms and laughing back there?"

"It's the Duck Principle."

Sands lifted his chin, asking.

Hitchcock grinned as he aimed his index finger with his thumb up at Sands in the manner of a handgun. "In duck season, we *shoot* ducks."

Sands looked down at his hands in his lap, nodding. "Lucky me," he said.

"Yeah, lucky you. And a lucky day for me as well."

Sands grinned and nodded at Hitchcock, rubbing his palms on his thighs again. "Right on."

† † †

RETURNING TO PACKARD in the booking room, Hitchcock held up the little red book. "I'd like to borrow this to show Allie, Ray."

Packard handed him several sheets of copy paper. "No can do, but knowing you'd ask, I copied all the pages."

He wrote a brief follow-up report for Packard before he left.

"See you day after tomorrow, and thanks for the 'A', that's how I like to start the new year," Packard said.

"Thanks for the copies. I'm glad you decided to lateral over from the University PD. Welcome aboard."

† † †

ALLIE HAD CHANGED to a loose-fitting dark blue V-neck sweater and khaki pants, her golden hair now in a ponytail. Hitchcock forgot why he came.

"Happy New Year," he said.

"Yes, happy new year to you too, honey. What happened at the station?"

"The station? The station. Oh yeah! Here!" He said, holding up the sheets of paper in his hand. "We found a little red address book in Sands's car. These are copies of the pages."

"Why would that be of interest to us?" she asked.

"Because we're in it."

"We?"

They sat on the couch as she read.

"This has to be the work of my ex's parents," she said. "Glendon's father, Horace, is a sort of king in terms of money and influence. He owns his own office building in downtown Seattle, and has others. He tried and failed to take Trevor from me in court last year."

"Well, he hasn't given up," Hitchcock said. "Your ex-father-in-law hired Tobias Olson, a Seattle private detective, to frame you as an unfit mother so they could take Trevor from you."

Allie nodded, staring at the floor, saying nothing.

"And Olson, being the waste of skin that he is," Hitchcock continued, "hired Sands, an ex-con on federal parole for bank robbery, to meet you so he could photograph you socializing with him to convince the court you're an unfit mother because you keep company with dangerous criminals."

She sighed and shook her head. "*How* would Olson find someone like Sands in the first place?"

"Birds of a feather..."

"What can I do? I can't fight him with no money."

"Didn't I catch Olson taking pictures of you?

"How could I forget?"

"Those pictures were to be evidence against you. Who has them now, us, or them?"

"Us," she replied, her hands fidgeting.

"Since you met Sands for coffee twice, there's bound to be more photos Olson took of you with him. But with Sands being caught and jailed in the middle of the operation, the photos they still have are no longer useful to them."

"Why not?"

"Because Sands was arrested while breaking into your car, at your apartment. His little red book contains evidence of a conspiracy against you because of whose names are in it. Olson and his client, your ex-father-in-law, can't risk his schemes being exposed to a judge.

They'll either give up or start over."

She scoffed. "My ex-father-in-law won't give up. Not until he gets what he wants—Trevor. So now what?"

"Now we wait."

"For what?"

"Their next move," Hitchcock replied. "Sands will call Olson from jail. Olson will panic. He'll be forced to change tactics. He won't tell MacAuliffe in order to keep the case. He can't afford to lose a client like MacAuliffe even in a good economy. In the meantime, we make you a harder target."

"How?"

"We move you and keep your new address a secret. There's a better place near here, nicer and more private."

Allie put her hand on his arm. "You make me feel protected, Roger."

He laid his head on her lap and looked up into her eyes, making kissing sounds. She giggled and gently slapped his chest. "Silly boy."

They kissed with abandon until he suddenly sat up.

"Moving you to a new place has another purpose besides protection," he said.

"What?" she asked, catching her breath.

"Tactics," Hitchcock said.

"Tactics?" she echoed, breathless.

"Olson must find another way to set you up if he is to keep the case going. Getting someone with a bad history next to you is the surest approach to having the court give him custody of Trevor. If we play our cards right, time is on our side."

Allie seemed relieved. "What's next, then?"

"Olson must find you first to save the case. Once he does, he'll watch you to learn what other changes you've made. Then he'll insert a new agent where you work at the Pancake Corral."

She nodded, hands resting on her lap. "Another question."

"What?" he asked, placing his hand on hers.

"You've never come here this early before. Your shift ended hours ago, so what happened that you came at this hour?"

"A little birdie told me you were in trouble."

"Be serious."

He hesitated, wondering what she would think if he told her about his strange ability. "I'm not like other people," he said. "I can see danger before it takes place. I was on my way home when suddenly I knew you were in danger, so I came."

"You can see the future?" she asked, incredulous.

"Only as it pertains to imminent threat. In the Army it kept me and those with me alive many times."

"How do you explain it? Where does it come from?"

He shrugged. "It's always been a mystery."

"I think I know."

"Tell me."

"Later," she said. "A request, if you please."

"Your wish is my command."

"Hold me."

CHAPTER FIVE
Day Shift, Day One

HITCHCOCK'S ALARM SOUNDED at 3:00 a.m. He listened to the rain outside and wished he had stayed in California. Forcing himself out of the warmth of his bed into the damp cold wasn't easy. He fed Jamie, showered, dressed, drank a protein shake. He touched the photograph of his dad on his nightstand as he left.

He and Otis were the first to arrive in the squad room. Sergeant Breen took the podium, rubbing his eyes as he watched the squad members file in front of him. As soon as they were seated, his gravelly pack-and-a-half-a-day voice read the latest bulletin out loud:

"'San Francisco Police Officer Harold Hamilton was shot and killed after responding to a bank robbery call at the Wells Fargo Bank at Seventh Avenue and Clement Street. When Officer Hamilton and his partner arrived, they attempted to enter the bank, and Officer Hamilton was shot and killed. Officer Hamilton's partner was able to return fire, wounding the suspect, who was arrested.

"At the officer's funeral, members of the Black Liberation Army planted a time bomb outside of the church. The bomb exploded but did not injure any of the mourners. Officer Hamilton had been a member of the San Francisco Police Department for six years and is survived by his wife and four children.'

BREEN'S EYES SCANNED the squad when he finished. "I read you this for a reason," he said. "Used to be that mornings were the hours when nothing happens. The bad guys were in jail or asleep, so when alarms went off as shops and stores open it was employee or owner error. We respond to nothing so many times that we become lax and lower our guard."

He paused and scratched the side of his blond crewcut. "But the times we're in are changing fast. Used to be that cop-killing was taboo in the underworld. No more. There are people out there now who want to kill us for political or social reasons or just for the sake of killing a cop.

"Take no alarm for granted, no matter how often they were false in the past. Pay attention to where their hands are, even the store employees you know. Changes in the way they talk or interact with you could be silent signals that something is wrong. As I just read, a quiet shift can explode in a split-second, and your life and the life of your loved ones can be shattered forever. If there're no questions, hit the bricks. Diss-*missed!*"

† † †

HITCHCOCK RADIOED IN service and headed for Eastgate. The radio was quiet. The festivities and heavy spending of the holidays were over. Tax time was around the corner. The streets glistened in the cold, steady drizzle, empty except for delivery trucks and newspaper boys on their routes.

The rain stopped as Hitchcock spotted a maroon Buick LeSabre in the rear lot of The Steak Out. He put his spotlight on the rear window, flooding the interior with light. The windows were fogged, indicating a body inside. He keyed his radio mic: "Checking out a red Buick LeSabre, Ocean David Sam. Five Two Three, Washington, behind The Steak Out, possibly occupied."

He approached along the passenger side, shining his flashlight into the interior. A man in his thirties, standard haircut, slacks and sport jacket, was slumped against the door in the driver's seat, mouth open, apparently asleep. The doors were locked, no key in the ignition, nothing on the seat next to him. When he saw the man breathing, Hitchcock rapped on the passenger side front door window with his eight-cell Kel-Lite flashlight.

"Police officer! Open the door!" he repeated twice, focusing on the man's hands.

He awoke with a start. Upon seeing Hitchcock, he rubbed his eyes and checked his watch. He leaned across the seat and opened the passenger door.

"Morning, officer," the man said.

Hitchcock smelled stale booze and bad breath.

"Good morning, sir. What's the situation here?"

The man rubbed his face with one hand, keeping the other on the steering wheel. "I met some friends here last night to listen to the new band." He paused to yawn. "At closing everyone wanted to go to an after-hours place in Seattle, but I had drunk too much to drive. I told them to go without me. I slept here. I think I'm okay now."

"You did right by not driving, sir. But before I let you drive, let's make sure you've slept it off. Hand me your driver's license and registration, then keep your hands where I can see them, please."

Without fumbling the man removed his wallet from his pants pocket and selected his driver's license and handed it to Hitchcock. He got his car registration from the glove box.

"Thank you, sir. Now please slide across the seat and step out."

Walker arrived by the time the man had passed four field sobriety tests with ease. He was clear of warrants. They watched him drive away.

"Guess what?" Walker asked, grinning like a kid who couldn't wait to tell a secret.

Hitchcock smiled knowingly. "You're hungry."

Walker gasped in fake shock. "How did you guess?"

"From the goofy grin on your mug and seeing that Art's is open now."

Walker tilted his head back and sniffed the air. "Ahhh," he said, exhaling. "I missed Art's food during our time on nights. I can smell the hot grease from here, calling me."

"It ain't food at Art's–it's grub. I'll call out for us."

"I already did."

"What if I arrested the guy in the Buick?"

"As your training officer for the past year, I knew you weren't going to arrest him before you did. If they need us, Dispatch has Art's phone number."

"You probably had Dispatch order for us too, so it would be waiting for us when we got there."

Walker chuckled. "Meet you there."

ART'S BURGER BAR was a classic '50s-vintage hole-in-the-wall American-style diner located a few yards off the frontage road. It shared a wall with Charlie's Place, the rough-and-tumble neighborhood tavern owned by Wally Evans.

They parked their cruisers at the door and walked in. Walker hitched his gun belt up around his thick muscular waist and grinned, rubbing his oversize hands together in eager expectation.

The tantalizing smells were almost visible, the sounds of thick slices of bacon, rows of link sausages, piles of shredded spuds sizzled and popped in their own way on the griddle, doughnut batter in round shapes hissing in vats of boiling grease and the rhythmic chugging of gallons of fresh coffee in a huge percolator created a sensory symphony of blue-collar breakfast in

JOHN HANSEN

the making.

They ordered, helped themselves to coffee and sat on chrome-legged chairs with red vinyl padded seats.

"Come 'n git it!" Art barked as two heavy porcelain platters clattered on the Formica counter.

Hitchcock checked for ashes in his food.

Walker pointed at his eggs. "Hey, Art, what're my eggs doing in all this grease? Heck, they're swimming in it."

Without a word, Art left the griddle, spatula in hand, dripping grease on the floor. Wearing a deadpan expression, he bent from the waist, eyeballing Walker's platter like a pool shark planning his next shot. Ash fell from the cigarette in his mouth to the counter. "The backstroke," he said without cracking a smile.

Hitchcock and Walker sauntered to their table with their plates, chuckling.

"Soldier boys," Art muttered, shaking his head but grinning as he ambled back to the griddle, spatula in hand, dripping more grease.

"Heard the latest about Forbes?" Walker asked as he bit off a hunk of bacon.

"He's not in trouble again, is he?"

"Just the opposite. He's not on the squad anymore."

"So I noticed," Hitchcock said.

Walker broke the yolks of his eggs with his fork, shook salt over them, and tasted his hash browns before he salted them while Hitchcock watched and waited.

"C'mon, cut the mystery."

"He got the job on the Warrant Detail for the next three months," Walker said, his mouth full.

"What? With his record of excessive force complaints? No way!"

Walker nodded. "No lie. He starts today."

"Something's not right." Hitchcock scowled. "The plum job most patrolmen want a turn at, Forbes gets?"

"I'm one of 'em, Roger. Plainclothes, regular hours, Monday through Friday, weekends off, a chance to work with a departmental legend like Brendan O'Rourke before he pulls the pin. And I'm not the only one with no citizen complaints who's been on the list going on two years."

Hitchcock shook his head.

"Why are you shaking your head? Forbes?'" Walker asked.

"Not Forbes—you. The work would drive a street warrior like you nuts in a week. Selecting arrest warrants from Records every morning, finding and arresting the wanted person at home or work. If they can't post bail, you take 'em to the county slammer. It's a perfect spot for an old caveman like O'Rourke with less than a year to go, but a problem child like Mark getting the job seems fishy."

"Very fishy," Walker agreed between mouthfuls of eggs over easy and crisp hash browns.

"Who's in charge of the Warrant Detail, anyway?"

"Guess."

"Just tell me," Hitchcock said irritably.

JOHN HANSEN

"Your not-so-secret enemy."

Hitchcock stared at Walker, holding his fork mid-air. "Bostwick?"

"Yup."

"Something's not right, Ira."

"Yup."

They ate in mutual silence.

"Arresting people on warrants isn't your bag. You're a born street cop," Hitchcock opined.

"Did you hear me say I wanted to make a career out of it? No. For me it'd be a nice break from rotating shifts every three months, and it would increase my chances for getting the next opening in the dicks."

† † †

TWO BURLY FLANNEL-SHIRTED men in their thirties made their way across the driveway from the Eastgate Motel. They yawned as they poured their coffee and ordered breakfast at the counter. Taking the nearest table, they smoked and chatted weather and sports with Hitchcock and Walker.

As more workingmen came in, Judy arrived, Art's only waitress, a blondish, lean, shapely looker, a raspy-voiced chain smoker in her mid-forties. Rumors had it that Judy was Art's squeeze. Greeting, teasing, and exchanging bawdy jokes and limericks with customers as she took their orders, she kept their coffee mugs full and their ashtrays empty.

Judy saw one of the truckers patting down stray hairs on his balding head. As she refilled his coffee, she said, *"I'd rather have Fingers than Toes. I'd rather have Ears than a Nose. And as for my Hair, I'm glad it's all there. I'll be awfully sad when it goes.'*

The truckers laughed uproariously. "Tell us another one!" They clamored. "C'mon, Judy!"

Grinning, Judy poured more coffee for the crowd she called "my Blue-Collar Brigade," set her coffee pot on a table, put her hands on her hips and said,

"There was a young girl from Rabat. Who had triplets: Nan, Pat, and Tat. It was fun in the breeding, but hell in the feeding, as she found she had no tit for Tat!'

Judy's customers pounded the tables with fists and open hands, laughing. The phone rang as Hitchcock and Walker laughed with them. "Station's calling for Walker!" Art yelled.

Hitchcock and Walker ran for the door. Walker radioed himself and Hitchcock back in service.

Dispatch advised: *"Silent alarm at the Mayfair store, 1510 145th Place Southeast."*

THE STORY OF the slain San Francisco officer was fresh on Hitchcock's mind as he sped to the scene. Walker positioned himself at the front corner of the store. Hitchcock covered the back. Walker used his binoculars to watch employees inside, bringing cash trays to the registers.

A delivery truck backed up to an open service door at the back. Hitchcock met the driver. "Wait a few, buddy. We're here on an alarm."

Walker came on the air. "I see employees working inside, Radio. Looks normal. Call the manager to come to the front door and let me in."

He approached the store on foot at an angle and peeked inside.

A chubby, baby-faced young man wearing a crisp, starched short-sleeved white shirt and red necktie opened the front door. "Officer, I am so sorry. I forgot to shut off the alarm when I arrived."

"Okay, but because the alarm went off, we're coming in to make sure everything is kosher," Walker said.

Hitchcock walked through the rear loading dock, checked the employees for ID, and for anyone hiding inside as Walker checked the offices, the safes and lectured the manager about proper alarm protocol.

The city was stirring when they cleared. Streets were filling with traffic, the volume increasing by the minute. Motorcycle units and accident investigation cars radioed that they were in service.

Otis came on the air: *One Zero Seven is en route to the station. Felony suspect in custody. Request the station team meet me when I arrive. Got a fighter on board.*

Hitchcock listened to calls coming in as he returned to Eastgate. Sherman and Brooks responded to a silent alarm at Bevan's Jewelers downtown. Traffic units responded to accident scenes. Dispatch sent Packard to a commercial burglary of a boat shop behind The Trunk Lid, the bar where a crowd mobbed Forbes when he tried to arrest a juvenile last fall.

† † †

HE DROVE BY the Pancake Corral after work. Allie's gray Toyota was there, as he expected. He checked the area for any occupied car in the vicinity, on surveillance. Nothing.

Satisfied that no one was on surveillance of Allie's apartment, he drove three blocks south, below Old Main Street, into an older neighborhood of narrow, tree-lined streets. He stopped at the place he was considering for Allie and studied the layout. *If I were to do surveillance on someone who lived here, how would I do it?* he asked himself.

Pleased with his find, he went to the manager's office.

CHAPTER SIX
The Measure of a True Officer

The Squad Room - 3:45 AM.

SERGEANT BREEN AT the podium, cigarette between his fingers, scowling as he flipped through the latest activity summaries. Hitchcock sat next to Otis, slurping hot instant coffee from the hall vending machine. The rest of the squad filed in, bleary-eyed.

Breen snuffed out his smoke and looked at his men. "Nothing happened last night except for two stolen cars, both taken from the Villa La Paz apartments up in Crossroads. Neither one was a repo. First up is a black '71 Ford Gran Torino, mag wheels, Ocean Paul George Six Nine One. Next is a metallic-gray '70 Oldsmobile 442, spoiler on the back, mag wheels, Tom Robert Tom Eight Four Seven. That's it, boys. Hit the bricks."

† † †

THE RADIO WAS dead quiet. Hitchcock made his usual sweeps of parking lots of bars and parks, followed by running license plates at the motels for warrants. No luck. By 5:00 a.m. officers began calling out at Sambo's in Midlakes or the Denny's near Crossroads for coffee, where they would chat and wait for calls.

To him the best hours for finding what the night shift missed were before sunrise. After sweeping the usual places, he probed the less-patrolled nooks and crannies of his beat, quickly poking in and out like a bloodhound sniffing along a trail.

He cruised along 118th Avenue SE south of the Wilburton train trestle. Past I-90 it was a seldom travelled two-lane asphalt ribbon hugged by dense woods on one side and swampland on the other that stretched for hundreds of yards to Lake Washington. His window was down. He tasted rain in the air and smelled Lake Washington before it came into view.

Here and there on either side of the road were remnants of old logging roads from a bygone era. Burlington-Northern railroad tracks, still in use, ran parallel to the east side of the road.

Fresh tire tracks in the mud of an old dirt road on his left caught his eye. The road turned right, disappearing into heavy brush. He U-turned, stopped on the shoulder, activated his four-way flashers, and got out for a closer inspection.

Two different tire widths and fresh tread patterns in the mud indicated a car and a truck entered hours ago.

Seeing from the tracks that only the truck came out, he walked in, carefully avoiding the delicate tire impressions. Barely out of sight from the road was the stolen black Ford Gran Torino described at shift briefing.

The glass had been smashed out. The license plates were in place, the hood was cold to the touch, the stereo, speakers, the tires and wheels had been removed. Footprints of different sizes trampled grass around the car indicated at least two or more people plundered it for saleable parts before they demolished it. Two-foot square imprints in the mud by each wheel indicated the suspects brought a square of plywood as a base to stabilize the jack in soft mud to safely remove the tires.

He radioed in his finding.

Sergeant Breen arrived minutes later.

"They want it to be found, Jack," Hitchcock said. "They drove it here, followed by someone in a truck. They stripped and trashed it, reported it stolen to collect on the insurance. They'll black market the tires, wheels and the stereo system next."

"Anything else?" Breen asked.

He pointed at the muddy areas where the wheels were removed. "We've got footprints of two, maybe three people. Even for three people, this took time."

He pointed at the smashed-out driver's door window. "They used the key to drive it here. A thief would've had to hot-wire it. This spells o-w-n-e-r. Maybe a relative or his wife helped, if she's still around."

"You learned a lot in the Seattle academy," Breen said approvingly. "Any other conclusions?"

"It'd take white-collar wages to qualify for a loan on a car like this. Unemployment benefits most likely ran out before the owner could get another job, so he turned to false reporting and fraud," Hitchcock speculated.

"Insurance money will keep the wolf from the door for a month or so, then what?" Breen asked.

"He probably fell behind on his payments and had to act before the repo men from the bank sucked it up in the dead of night."

"I'll get the dicks out here to process it," Breen said.

"I did well at casting molds in the academy. This is my first chance to do it for real."

"Go for it, Roger. There's rain in the forecast."

† † †

USING THE CASTING kit in the trunk of his cruiser, he made wood frames around the clearest footprints, and truck and car tire tracks. He mixed Plaster of Paris powder and distilled water in a plastic bowl until it was the consistency of pancake batter. He poured the mix slowly over a plastic spatula to deflect the force of the pour from disturbing the fine tread details.

When the mix was an inch deep, he laid in strips of metal wire mesh for strength, and added more mix until the mesh was covered. Using a twig, he scratched the date, case and evidence numbers on each cast before it dried. He laid the casts in shallow cardboard boxes lined with newspaper and set them in the trunk of his patrol car and took them to the evidence room.

A gusty rainstorm picked up as he left the station. He transferred his badge to his winter coat and opened the side slits for access to his revolver and baton and resumed his drive to Newport Shores.

THE NEWPORT MARINA was a rustic, eclectic setting. Its weathered wooden docks jutted into the lake like the stubby fingers of an old man. It was home to canoes, kayaks, sailboats, cabin cruisers and speedboats. The office was a standalone cabin near the docks. A stone's throw from the office was the dark brown rambler where the manager and his wife lived.

It's remote location, a long, lonely drive through the woods, was the reason most cops overlooked this haven for summer drinking and drug parties. Thefts of boats, boating equipment and trailers happened year-round. It was a lesser-known hideout for not only derelicts, cheating husbands kicked out of the house by their wives, but runaways and fugitives from justice also found safe harbor in cars or boats, theirs or someone else's, with or without owner permission.

Another type of illegal activity was afoot that no one on the right side of the law yet knew about.

✝ ✝ ✝

WIND-DRIVEN RAIN pelted the office as Hitchcock made his way to the door. The man who met him was in his fifties, a ruddy-cheeked sort, his receding hairline matched the shade of his heavy gray wool Cardigan sweater with brown leather buttons. He smiled at the sight of Hitchcock in uniform.

"Good morning, sir. I stopped by to introduce myself. I'm on morning shift for the next three months. Except for my days off on Tuesdays and Wednesdays I'm the one you'll meet if you need us before noon."

"Tuesdays and Wednesdays are horrible days off! My sympathies, officer. Glad to meet you, though. I'm Wilbur Jenkins, by the way. Won't you come in from the cold? We got fresh coffee on."

"Thanks, I'll have to take a rain-check. I'm Roger Hitchcock, and I'm pleased to meet you."

Jenkins's face broke into a warm smile as he shook Hitchcock's hand. "So, you're Officer Hitchcock! The wife and I read about you quite a bit in the newspaper, young man. Glad to meet you. Stop by anytime for a cup with me and the wife, coffee's always on."

"Thanks, Mr. Jenkins, I'll take you up on it."

"Call me Wilbur. Everyone does."

CHAPTER SEVEN
A Touch of Chivalry

WITH THE SATISFACTION of a productive first day under his belt, Hitchcock went for a one mile run with Jamie on the backroads of Wilburton Hill, breathing in the moist, cool Northwest air. It pleased him that his wind had improved since he stopped smoking. He showered, dressed in pressed jeans, slipped a tan pullover sweater over his off-duty .38, and touched the photo of his father on his nightstand as he left.

Bill Chace, the ever-cheerful owner of the Pancake Corral seated him and brought him coffee. "Allie's getting off work in a minute, Hitch."

Allie's face beamed when she saw him. "This is a pleasant surprise, honey, what's up?"

"Leave your car here. I have something to show you."

"Okay, but Mom's with Trevor, I can't keep her waiting too long."

He drove her seven blocks north of the Corral to a

dark brown, wood-sided, four-plex, secluded in a grove of firs and cedars, below and out of view of, 104th Avenue, the noisy main drag.

He led her up the stairs and unlocked the door. Allie gasped as she walked into a spacious living room, brown brick fireplace, updated kitchen and appliances, fresh paint, new carpet and drapes, two bedrooms, two baths and a balcony.

"Well, what do you think?" he asked.

"It's beautiful, but I can't afford something like this."

"It's less than you're paying at the Bay Vue."

"Come on! How could that be?"

"The manager is a former high school classmate. We played varsity baseball together."

"How did you find this place?"

"Us cops know our town. You'll be safer here. Not only is it hard to find, but you'll still be also on the second floor, closer to the police station and work. The covered parking under the building makes it harder for a surveillance man to keep an eye on your car."

HE PAID THE rent deposit for her. They spent the next three hours making trips with the bed of his El Camino overflowing with boxes and furniture. They unpacked and set everything up.

To prevent Olson or anyone working for him from finding Allie through utilities or phone records, he opened new accounts for her in his name, using his post office box for her mailing address.

"This is your new phone number," he said, giving her a slip of paper. "The only weak link is that you can be followed here from work," he warned as he unpacked the last box of dishes.

"Keep an eye out for cars following you. Don't go straight to work from home or straight home from work. Take a detour, pull over and wait. That will expose anyone who's following you. Drive to the police station. No one will follow you there."

"What about my ex? Glendon has visitation rights."

"Always comply with court orders. Given recent events, your new number will be unlisted," he replied. "Give your ex only your work phone number. Tell him you moved, but not where to. The next move is theirs."

Allie's stare stopped him cold.

"What?" he asked.

"This won't go over well with them–they can make people disappear," she said.

He scoffed. "Your ex is a pussy."

"I wasn't referring to Glendon," she said.

"Explain."

She looked down, shook her head once and said nothing.

He paused, looking at her. Her eyes were aimed at the floor.

"Okay, Allie," he said, "I get it that your ex-father-in-law is a rich, powerful man who is used to getting what he wants. I accept that such people could have underworld connections. If that's the case here, then know this—they can hunt *you* down any time they want to. They can make *you* disappear and then, God forbid, take Trevor legally."

"I know," Allie said somberly.

46

CHAPTER EIGHT
Last-Ditch Efforts

ALLIE'S COMMENT ABOUT her former in-laws making people disappear dominated his thoughts as his El Camino rumbled down the long, narrow gravel road to his cabana in the woods.

He rounded up the asphalt driveway at the end of the road to find Rhonda Kringen M.D. waiting in her Suburban.

She rolled her window down. "Can we talk?"

"Sure," he said, gesturing toward the cabana. *She must have just gotten off shift at the ER*, he thought when he noticed her hospital scrubs under her jacket.

She lingered with hope in her eyes after he slid open the cabana door. He motioned her to the couch. She sat, wistful, hands clasped in her lap. He took a chair across from her and looked at her kindly, waiting.

"Roger," she began, "I am *so sorry* about the way my guests treated you at the Christmas party at my place. After you left, I sent everyone home. I've come to get you back—"

"You're not to blame," he interrupted. "I'm glad things happened the way they did."

Her jaw dropped. "You're *what*?"

"The behavior of your friends opened my eyes to the fact that I'm an outsider, a trespasser. They circled their wagons around you like old-time settlers did to protect their own against Indian raiders. I bear no grudges. No one is to blame—you, least of all."

Silence held the room for several seconds. "Have I lost you, Roger?" she asked, her voice barely above a whisper, tears beading in her eyes.

"It's for the best," he said gently, "because now I understand how far apart our worlds are. Even if I finished medical school and became an MD, I wouldn't be friends with people like them. If we married and I remained in police work, you wouldn't fit into my world, among cops and cop wives."

She burst into tears. "How do you know I wouldn't? You never gave me a chance! I could because I love you so much. This isn't fair of you!" she sobbed.

Searching his mind for a tactful reply, he said, "Let me tell you a true story I've told no one else. Want to hear it?"

"Please," she said, wiping her eyes.

"As you know, I served in Phu Loi, a sort of ER in the jungle, on my first tour," he began, "the lieutenant in charge of enlisted medics was an MD from Maryland. He befriended several of us who were from the West in particular. We didn't know at first that he believed himself and others of his class to be superior to us, but later it came out.

"One night someone in our unit acquired some American whiskey, which we shared with the officers. As the booze lowered our inhibitions, the lieutenant's true side came out. He said cruel and ugly things about us enlisted men, about his patients who were wounded soldiers, and the poor Vietnamese peasants we helped on the sly, out of compassion. He even mimicked some of us.

"I had been drinking too, so my inhibitions were lowered. His cruelty and hypocrisy so enraged me that I went after him. He knew of my boxing career. He ran and hid behind others, begging for protection. It took two strong men, a sergeant and a corporal, to keep me from taking him out... I'd be in prison today if I'd gotten to him."

"What a terrible individual for you to have to work for," Rhonda sniffled.

"Over time, I came to understand that mocking was the lieutenant's way to mask his fears of being in a war zone. Because we faced dangers he couldn't, he hated us. He hated me for exposing him as a coward when I tried to give him the beating he deserved in front of everyone."

Taking a tissue from her pocket, Rhonda wiped her eyes, then her nose. "I wish you had beaten him. It might have straightened him out."

"From then on, he never pretended to like any of us," he continued, "even his fellow officers avoided him. Except when our medical duties required, he and I never spoke again."

"I had no idea. I've never been around anything like that," Rhonda sympathized, still sniffling.

"The attitudes and behavior of your guests brought that lieutenant back for me. Alcohol lowered their masks and exposed who they really are and what they really think. I left the party because I realized our worlds will never meet."

She stood up after a few seconds. "I'll let myself out. Can we say goodbye like we said hello, with a kiss?"

He stood, put his hands on her shoulders and they kissed. Rhonda held him for long seconds, pressing herself into him.

"We don't have to break up. Come back to me," she pleaded, whispering, longing in her voice.

Unexpected feelings of guilt regarding Allie filled his mind. He stepped back, breaking the embrace.

Rhonda sighed and dropped her gaze. Her hands fell to her sides. "It's goodbye, then. I will always love you," she said, regret in her voice.

He had no mixed feelings about letting her go as he walked her to her Suburban. Passion for her was never there for him. He assumed love would develop over time. He had peace as he stood in the driveway, watching her Suburban until it was out of sight.

The re-reading Stephen Crane's *Red Badge of Courage*

he planned would have to wait. His body demanded sleep. He stretched out on his bed. Then, without thinking about it, he reached for his phone and dialed Allie's new phone number.

"Hello?" The sound of her voice pleased him.

"Me here. Before I go to sleep, I want to remind you to constantly check to see if anyone is following you. Next week, I'm going to teach you to shoot."

"I'm up for it, honey. My dad and my brothers hunted deer and elk a lot. Tuesday and Wednesday are my days off, same as you."

"Tuesday morning, then. Bye."

"Goodnight, Roger, sweet dreams, and thank you."

SEATTLE PRIVATE INVESTIGATOR Tobias Olson slammed his phone down and pounded his desk with his fist, shouting unprintable curses. His secretary came running in.

"What's wrong, Toby?"

"I'm ruined, Susie! Ruined!"

"Wh-what? I thought the case was going so well."

Olson groaned, leaned forward in his chair and put his head between his hands. "Sands called me collect," he said, "from jail. He got arrested by the Bellevue cops, at Allison Malloy's apartment on New Year's Day."

Susie's mouth fell open. "Oh no, Toby. How did it happen?"

"He didn't tell me all the details. What he did tell

was bad enough to kill the operation. Sands is in jail for multiple charges, including being a felon in possession of a firearm."

"That's bad," she said. "Sands is finished."

"He is—his parole will be revoked. Its back to prison for him. He said he told the cops nothing. I sure hope he didn't."

"What now?"

"My situation is desperate. I've got to change tactics to save the case. More Boeing layoffs are coming, the economy will collapse further. Without Mr. MacAuliffe as my client, I won't be able to stay in business."

"We need another like Sands. Better a woman next time," Susie said.

Olson stared at her. "Why a woman?"

"Because Allison's a woman, for one thing, who is dating a cop. No man will be able to get near her or even want to try with a cop in the picture. Women are less threatening. The right woman can get close enough to Allison to get the results you need."

"I see your point," Olson acknowledged, rubbing his hands together as he always did when in the grip of anxiety. "But first I have to Little Miss Waitress. I hope she hasn't moved, which is likely after Sands got himself arrested at her apartment. Once I know where she is, we'll find another undercover agent who can do a better job than Sands did of setting her up as an unfit parent.

"We'll need someone with a long criminal history, yet who is smooth enough to get close to Allison in spite of Hitchcock hanging around."

"Hitchcock?" Susie asked.

"Yeah, Hitchcock," Olson grumbled. "Why?"

"The name rings a bell. Just to confirm my understanding, Toby—is this Hitchcock the cop who caught you photographing her and confiscated your film?"

"Uh-huh," Olson nodded, looking at her.

"Isn't he the one who shot and killed a drug dealer last fall? It was in the paper?"

"One and the same. I warned Sands about him, ex-boxer, decorated war veteran, recently killed a negro in a gunfight. I even gave him a news photo of Hitchcock so he'd be safe. Sands bragged that he could handle him. Hah! So much for *that!*"

"If Sands had a photo of Hitchcock on him when he was arrested, it would be a deal-breaker for you, Toby," Susie said as she returned to her front office.

Olson slammed his fist on his desk again. "Damn me!" he shouted at the top of his voice.

Susie rushed back into Olson's office. "What?"

"I forgot to ask Sands the arresting officer's name," he explained. "If it was Hitchcock, and Sands told him *anything*, the MacAuliffes will move on, and I'm out of business!"

"There's always the bail bond companies," she said. "You've lots of good contacts with them."

Olson shook his head. "I'm too old and fat to be a bounty hunter. It's dangerous work."

"What about the defense attorneys you know? They've always got work."

"The best of the bunch have their own investigators. The pay is chicken feed, but it's worth a try," he said as he put on a brown, beat-up fedora hat, scuffed shoes worn down at the heel, and slipped into his tattered trench coat, the one he used in undercover roles, playing a poor down-and-out old-timer.

"The Rolodex on my desk has the names of defense attorneys I've worked for in the past. Look them up and offer our services."

Taking his camera bag, battered black leather briefcase and a cane, he told Susie, "I'm out of the office for the next couple days. I'll call you to check my messages."

"I'll hold the fort down while you're away."

"Thanks. Say, Susie, isn't your kid sister about to be released from prison?"

"June gets out on parole next week. Why?"

CHAPTER NINE
Betrayal Brewing

LIEUTENANT BOSTWICK SHUT his office door before he continued his phone conversation. He pressed the receiver tight against his ear and covered his mouth with his other hand. The discussion wasn't going well.

"As I explained to you twice already," he told his caller. "Chief Carter rejected my suggestion that we create a review board just for this incident. They decided to rely on the coroner's inquest instead. That's what Seattle P.D. does and they always follow Seattle's lead."

"Then we'll discredit Chief *Cahtah* for not having a review board. Ghost-write an editorial for us, *Bahstwick*. We'll put someone else's name on it and our contacts in the papers will print it," the caller said in his sneering nasal New England accent. "Work up a 'citizen' letter campaign to trash the chief and the *Depahtment* for reckless *disregawd* for citizen safety."

"Uh, yeah, but—" Bostwick began.

"No buts about it, *Bahstwick*. You did one of those

for us last year, as I recall. A job well done."

"I am *Lieutenant* Bostwick, and the letter campaign you had me do backfired because of citizen outrage in defense of the Chief and the officer who fired his gun at a fleeing burglar."

"*Whatevah.* This *Depahtment* is small *potaytas, Bahstwick.*"

"Given the favorable press Hitchcock and Sherman received for the way they handled the shooting they were in," Bostwick said, "what you propose would be disastrous for us. And in case you aren't aware, the shooting involving Hitchcock and Sherman became old news last week when a patrol sergeant stopped two wanted felons from escaping by blowing up their car with a shotgun."

"Listen to me, *Bahstwick.* Your job is to undermine the *Depahtment.* Ours is to persuade the public they need a new chief. Together we remold the *Depahtment* the way *we* want it. You are aware of our policy of ridding the *Depahtment* of any officer who is involved in a shooting, no matter how justified. Even if they are cleared, we want them out. *Veterans* especially. If they won't leave, we shame and discredit them and pass them over for promotion until they go. Other city and state governments are starting to do the same, but with discretion, so the citizens don't find out."

"Oh—so I'm supposed to keep targeting Hitchcock and Sherman?"

"Of *course,*" the caller sneered. "Begin a campaign to

discredit the officers we want out. Hitchcock and Sherman in particular. Exploit any crisis that comes along. Create one if one doesn't happen on its own. The possibilities are endless. Find things you can write them up for. Violations of policy. Anything. No matter how minor."

"Hitchcock and Sherman are much harder to discredit now because they were not only cleared for the shooting, but they've also been *honored* for it," Bostwick said. "Regarding those two, we'd best lay low for a while."

"They aren't the only ones we want out. You know who the others are. Focus on them for now."

"Understood. My newest man on the inside is close to the others, he's my mole in the ranks," Bostwick confided in a low voice. "Allow him time. He's my mouse in the corner."

"Talk soon, *Bahstwick*," the third-floor man said, his nasal voice dripping contempt as he hung up.

After the call, Bostwick told the duty sergeant. "I'm going to a lunch meeting. Be back about three-thirty."

† † †

BOSTWICK STEPPED OUTSIDE as the Warrant Detail's black '68 Ford Fairlane with black sidewall tires and spotlights mounted on each fender backed into the prisoner loading bay by the station door.

As he had seen generals do in old late night war movies on tv, Bostwick stood at parade rest, feet shoulder-width apart, hands behind his back, chin up, wearing aviator sunglasses and a sneer.

The Department legend, six-foot-six, scowling hard-knuckled, aging Irish brawler, Brendan O'Rourke, unfolded himself out of the driver's seat.

Bostwick acknowledged the giant with a timid nod, but the fierce, independent O'Rourke snorted and shook his head in an open show of disrespect. He refused to acknowledge a cowardly backstabber as unworthy of his badge and uniform as Bostwick.

O'Rourke respected very few people on the Department. His new partner, Mark Forbes, wasn't one of them. He regarded Forbes as a conceited, insecure, adolescent pussy whose top priority was spending hours in a fancy gym, working out in front of a mirror, packing on slabs of useless muscle instead of meeting the needs of his wife and kids.

Forbes opened the rear door, unlocked the wrist and leg chains, grabbed the prisoner by the arm and yanked him out of the back seat. The prisoner, a slender, spectacled, middle-aged desk-jockey type, bore the usual signs of having been roughed up.

From behind O'Rourke put a huge hand on Forbes's arm just above the elbow and squeezed. Nothing needed to be said. Fearing O'Rourke's reputation as a barroom brawler and bareknuckle prizefighter in his youth, Forbes eased up on the prisoner. And Bostwick, the make-believe general, strolled away to his car.

CHAPTER TEN
The Imposters

A YOUNG CHINESE waitress scurried to the back the second she saw Bostwick strutting toward The Great Wall. Customers snickered and scoffed at his imperial walk and wearing dark aviator sunglasses indoors. Juju came out from the back, smiling, radiating lust and power, beauty and mystery in the way of the Orient, dressed to reveal her sensuality, seduction in her smile.

"Come to my spessal room, boss-man, I take care of you," she said, bowing and smiling. She led Bostwick by the hand to her private room. She barked orders in Mandarin to another waitress who ran into the kitchen. Juju shut the door and slid her arms around Bostwick's, neck, kissing him so fully his heart raced and his head almost popped.

Before Juju, Bostwick had never dated, even once. So sheltered his life had been that he couldn't resist the allure of a beautiful, sensuous foreigner with an exotic accent, a woman of another race, whose past was colorful, steamy and mysterious. Juju brought spice and adventure to his Styrofoam life, filtered by his parents. She had sunk her hooks into him. Deep.

To impress Juju with his importance, Bostwick wore his uniform and gun belt when he saw her, even off duty. Over time he came to believe his own lies about himself as a romantic swashbuckler in the mold of movie stars Errol Flynn or Clark Gable.

Delusions of grandeur changed his walk from a stoop-shouldered shuffle to a swagger. He would have been infuriated if he knew that the younger officers mimicked his imitation military strut for laughs during their rowdy post-shift drinking sessions.

He realized his fantasies were leading him toward a terrible dilemma. He yearned to marry Juju, but his parents, who were white, wealthy East Coast elitists, kept a disdainful distance from people of other races and whites who didn't come from a long heritage of wealth and privilege. Though he was their only child, he knew they would disinherit him if they found out about Juju.

Bostwick couldn't stop himself if he wanted to. The thrill of a clandestine affair with such an exotic beauty as Juju, running huge risks for her, blurred the lines between reality and fantasy, numbing him from any lasting thoughts of the consequences he would face sooner or later. More and more he saw himself as a gallant, battle-hardened warrior of rank, the scourge of communist hordes.

† † †

AS A SHE-PANTHER takes her prey to her den to devour it, so Juju led Bostwick to her private office. As a former prostitute, she discerned Bostwick's juvenile fantasies and used them to her advantage. She put his hat on her head, slid her arms around his neck and kissed him.

He melted when she purred in his ear: "So, you got my infahmayshun, my Rowlie-sahn?"

Red-faced and burning with desire, he handed her a slip of white folded paper from his pocket. "Here it is," he said, his voice husky with emotion. Any guilt he may have felt over his latest and deepest betrayal of a fellow officer vanished in a cloud of boyish lust. He hadn't yet realized that he was addicted to Juju. She was his heroin.

"So, tell me, what else new at po-lees station now, man-boss?" she asked as she pocketed the white slip of paper, removed his glasses and clip-on necktie and stroked his flaccid face while loosening his collar.

Made weak from a sheltered life, Bostwick lacked the savvy to recognize and resist the charms of a ruthless woman. Defenseless and self-deceived as he was, he disclosed all he knew about the Department's inner workings, current gossip, naming his contacts on the third floor, and his enemies, not knowing that Juju was recording everything.

† † †

TOBIAS OLSON PANICKED when he didn't find

Allie's car at the Pancake Corral or the Bay Vue Apartments. *If she's moved, her job at the Pancake Corral would be the only way to locate her, or did she quit that too?*

The drapes were wide open, adding to his fears. Using his cane to augment his disguise, he cautiously climbed the stairs, faking his need of the cane for support. As he feared, the apartment was empty. He faked leaning on his cane as he went downstairs to the manager's office.

"What a lovely apartment building this is," Olson said, laying on the fake cordiality. "I wonder if there is a unit available?"

"Yes, sir. Want to see it?" offered the manager, a man in his sixties with thinning gray hair and silver wire rim glasses, whom everyone called Buddy.

"Please, I need to move. Going through a dee-vorce," Olson said in a sorrowful tone, putting on a hurt expression, leaning on his cane.

Buddy showed him a ground floor one-bedroom unit. "This one's ready. Cleaned, repainted, new carpet, one-bedroom. Got a great view of the lake, too."

"Actually, I prefer a second-floor unit if one is available."

"Well, sir, one became vacant a couple days ago. Two bedrooms, but it ain't ready for new tenants just yet."

Olson paused as he stared out the large window at the lake.

"Having two-bedrooms would give me storage

space. May I see it, even if it isn't ready?"

Olson hobbled on his cane upstairs behind Buddy to Allie's former apartment.

"Ah, *this* is much nicer. A superior view of the lake, and of course, more room. Why would anyone leave such a perfect spot? Did she say?"

"No sir. The gal who lived before is a single mom. She moved out after the cops arrested a rough character in the parking lot a few days ago."

"Huh, rough character, you say. Was she involved with him?"

Buddy shrugged. "She's a single mom, like I said. Always paid her rent on time. Didn't date anybody. Pretty little thing, never any trouble."

"She left quickly after the cops came, though. Strange, don't you think?"

Buddy shrugged again but made no reply.

"Thanks for showing me this unit. I'll be looking at one more place before I decide. I'll call you."

"Thanks, mister. Say, would you give me your name in case you call when I'm not here?"

Olson turned to Buddy as he stepped outside. "Sure. Turner's the name. Frank Turner."

"Do you have a card or a phone number so I can call you when this unit is ready or if a better unit becomes available, Mr. Turner?"

Shaking his head and looking down, feigning sorrow, Olson replied, "Sorry, but at the moment I don't. It's the dee-vorce, you know."

† † †

OLSON RETURNED TO his office and dialed his contact at Puget Power.

"Looks like she terminated her service in Bellevue two days ago, Toby" his contact said, "No record of her opening a new account so far, and we cover everywhere outside Seattle. I'll watch for her opening a new account with us. You might try Seattle City Light. If she's not there, maybe she moved in with somebody."

Olson called his nephew at Seattle City Light. No record of Allison. His contact at the Postal Inspector's office also came up empty-handed for a forwarding address for Allison. He *had* to locate her if he was to save his client relationship with Horace MacAuliffe. His last hope of keeping the case would involve following her from the Pancake Corral, *if* she still worked there, to where she moved to. Then he would plot anew.

† † †

HITCHCOCK'S HOME PHONE rang. "Hi, Roger. Patty in Records here. Buddy Shaw of the Bay Vue Apartments is asking for you to call him right away."

Buddy answered on the first ring. "It was just like you said, Officer Hitchcock. A man came by trying to find Allie less than a half hour ago."

"How would you describe him?"

"About sixty, five-ten, overweight, double chin, glasses. Walks with a cane. His trench coat's seen better days, same for his crappy short-brim hat with a feather in the band."

Olson, of course, Hitchcock thought with a smile. "What did he do?"

"He went upstairs to Allie's old place first. He peeked in the window, then he came to my office. 'Going through a dee-vorce,' he says. Needs a new pad."

"Then what happened?"

"I tested him by showing him a ground floor one-bedroom unit, but, no surprise, he said he wanted an upstairs apartment. I showed him Allie's place. Instead of asking about the rent, he tried to pump me for information about the last tenant. I knew he was the guy you expected to come around. Can you guess how?"

Pleased by Buddy's enthusiasm, he asked, "How?"

"He asked me why 'she' would leave such a nice place."

Olson, the oaf in sheep's clothing, Hitchcock mentally joked.

"Wanna know what else?"

"Yes. What?" Hitchcock asked, smiling.

"I pretended not to notice his slip—like it went over my head, so I don't think he's aware he made it."

"I'm very impressed, Mr. Shaw! What happened next?"

Buddy waxed proud as he went on. "Well, sir, I could tell he considers himself a smooth operator, but I had him figured out."

"How's that?"

"First off, I saw him go up the stairs holding the cane

in his left hand when he first arrived. He leaned on it with his right hand when he came downstairs to my office, favoring his right leg. Struck me as odd that a guy with a cane wants to use stairs. I climbed the stairs with him. He moved slowly, using the cane. I told him the former tenant moved away after a guy got arrested in the parking lot. That got him asking questions, but I played dumb. I asked him his name in case he called back. He said, 'Frank Turner,' but I didn't believe him, especially when he switched sides and limped down the stairs with his left hand. So, I got the plate number of his car."

"Outstanding work, Buddy!" Hitchcock exclaimed. "Did you do police work in the past?"

A question like that coming from a real cop thrilled Buddy. "No, sir. Professional bookkeeping is what I did for most of my working life. I'm semi-retired now."

"So how did you know to do all this?"

"Cop shows."

"Cop shows?"

"Yeah. *Dragnet*, Sergeant Joe Friday, 'Just the facts, ma'am,' and *Adam 12, Highway Patrol. Perry Mason*, too."

"Before we hang up, Buddy, I'll need the plate number of the guy's car."

CHAPTER ELEVEN
The Pusher Man

Tuesday - 3:00 P.M.
Chevron Station
Lake Hills Shopping Center

UNTIL NOW THE day had been a normal workday for Randy Fowler. He changed oil and lubing fittings of customers' cars under the lube rack, a hydraulic hoist, looking sharp in clean white overalls bearing the Standard Oil emblem.

The weather was its usual drab, cloudy and cool self—unremarkable in every detail. The only sounds were neighborhood traffic on 156th Avenue and Lake Hills Boulevard, kids walking home from school, and the ringing of the bell when customers drove up to the gas pumps.

Randy had been on the mend since Hitchcock saved him from death by heroin overdose a year ago. He had regained the right kind of weight, was clear-headed, clean-cut looking and making good money working full-time at the neighborhood gas station.

A byproduct of his recovery and being the oldest son was his family acknowledging him as the head of the household. His father committed suicide years earlier. Since completing rehab and working full-time, he used most of his income to pay the household bills, which relieved his mother of having to work two jobs.

RANDY SUDDENLY SENSED a powerful presence of evil. He turned around. Leaning against the driver's door of a metallic green Pontiac Firebird, arms folded, a cocky smirk on his face, stringy blond hair to the shoulders, was Mike Smith. He stared at Randy as a wolf eyes a sheep it is about to take down.

His mind flashed back to scenes of Smith getting him high, first on marijuana, then coaxing him into harder drugs when he was high, his brushes with death, the emergency room, the agony of withdrawal, what his family went through to save him. He turned his back on Smith, continuing his work.

"Got a big load of smack, and black tar too," Smith said, ending the tense silence. "Got it in my car."

"I'm clean now," Randy said, focusing on his work, wishing Smith would leave.

Smith waited in silence like the predator he was.

"You heard what happened to Guyon, right?" Randy said as he wiped oil from his hands with a shop rag.

"Who hasn't?" Smith scoffed. "The pig Hitchcock smoked him. So?"

"What do you mean, 'so'?"

"Hitchcock got rid of my competition for me. I'm taking over Guyon's operation. I'm offering you a deal."

"What kinda deal?"

Smith gestured to his Firebird, a gleaming new metallic green muscle car with custom mag wheels, raised white lettering on the tires. "Dig my car, man? It's new. Paid cash. Sit in the driver's seat like I'm showing you a problem I'm having."

Randy sat down. Smith reached under the dash and brought out a handful of small balloons containing white powder.

"It's been stepped on only once," Smith said, "with powdered sugar. If you want in, you can cut it again."

Randy's eyes bulged with amazement when Smith opened the center console where he had a large plastic bag almost full of off-white powder. "It hasn't been cut yet," he said.

"I don't want to go to jail."

"No sweat," Smith said. "The Bellevue pigs got no narcs, only uniforms and regular detectives. They don't have a clue what's going on right under their noses."

Randy held his silence.

"*C'mon, man!* You can make more money with me than workin' on people's cars like a flunky."

Randy paused, staring out the windshield of Smith's Firebird. "Payday is day after tomorrow." He sighed. "I'll be here at this same time then. Gotta get back to work. Boss is watching me."

† † †

HITCHCOCK'S PHONE RANG. "Hi Roger. Patty in Records. A guy named Rooster called, asking for you to call him right away at this number."

Randy answered before the first ring completed. "Roger, here's the number for the pay phone at the Mayfair store. Call me in two minutes. I'm at work and I can't talk here."

He called the number. "What's up, Randy?"

"Mike Smith just left. He showed me a lot of heroin, some in balloons under the dash of his car and he's got black tar."

"Describe the car."

"Green Firebird. Loud pipes. New. Big emblem on the hood. Mag wheels."

"Anyone with him?"

"Nope."

"How does he know where you work?"

"I'm wondering that myself."

"What else went on?"

"I told him I get paid day after tomorrow. He said he'd be here."

"Where is Smith most likely to sell dope?"
"Robinswood Park, mostly."

CHAPTER TWELVE
No Time to Lose

IF HITCHCOCK KNEW anything about the ways of Mike Smith, it was that he would be selling heroin to kids as fast as he could. Young lives would be damaged forever unless he moved fast.

Sergeant Martin Conrad didn't have a squad of his own. He was on permanent rotation, filling in for other Patrol sergeants on their days off, which spoke volumes about his standing with the Brass. He was Hitchcock's supervisor on Sergeant Breen's two days off.

Conrad was known among the Department's rank-and-file for doing just enough to get by, for his indifference to them and citizens alike. None of the Patrol officers Hitchcock knew respected Conrad. His frequent visits to Lieutenant Bostwick's office added to their distrust of him.

Hitchcock's better judgment told him the rumors were true—that Conrad, a married man, stole small amounts of marijuana from the evidence room to use with his new girlfriend, a topless dancer at The Bavarian Gardens, formerly the Sunset Drive-in located on the outskirts of town. The rumors came from more than one source, they were consistent, yet Conrad had never been investigated, as if someone higher up protected him.

Hitchcock disliked and distrusted Conrad for reasons of his own. Whatever shift he was on, Conrad followed him around Eastgate on the days he filled in for Sergeant Breen.

But dislike and distrust must take a back seat to a large amount of heroin on the street, intended for minors.

Hitchcock met Conrad car-to-car in the field and briefed him.

Conrad was tall, gangly and long-faced, pale and bald as an egg. He furrowed his brows as he listened to Hitchcock.

"Exactly who are you getting this from?"

"A reliable informant I've used before."

"I want to assess the reliability of the information and know its source before I release it. Who is this so-called informant?"

"Someone who has given me reliable information before about the drug scene."

"You're barely off probation and you're defying me, your supervisor, Hitchcock. Don't be stupid."

"I won't name my informant and you shouldn't ask me to. The situation we face is urgent. What I'm giving you could save lives if you simply release it to Patrol,

Traffic and detectives to be on the lookout for Smith and his vehicle."

Conrad glared at Hitchcock. His knuckles turned white as he gripped his steering wheel. "Tell me who the person is, or I'll write you up for insubordination. Getting a search warrant based on unsubstantiated information could get us sued."

Hitchcock scoffed and shook his head. "I never said anything about a search warrant. There's no known address. We're sounding the alert for a known heroin dealer who is at large in our town, selling hard drugs to minors. All we have is a car description. Probable Cause exists to at least make a stop, which could lead to an arrest. Sergeant Breen knows about the reliability of my informants."

"But I don't, so tell me who it is."

"Why don't you call Jack at home if you don't believe me?"

"I'll have to write you up for insubordination."

"Go ahead, write me up, Martin, and you'll be explaining to the Brass why I see your personal car so often at the back of The Great Wall and at The Hilltop, and your unexplained absences when you supervise our squad on Jack's days off. They'll be interested in the dates and times I've got in my notes, and there's more that I haven't mentioned."

Conrad clenched his jaw as he stared out his windshield, put his car in gear and drove away without another word.

† † †

BEFORE THE NOON shift change, Conrad sneaked into the evidence room where he pocketed two ounces of marijuana he took from a sealed evidence envelope. He headed for his car to stash the dope there. He looked forward to getting high with Delilah, the stage name of his exotic dancer girlfriend, as soon as he got off work.

A pudgy man in his thirties, dressed in baggy green corduroy pants and a slept-in gray sweatshirt, approached Conrad as he unlocked his car.

"Are you Sergeant Martin Conrad?"

"I am. What can I do for you?"

"I'm a process server, and you are served." He handed an envelope to Conrad and walked away.

He scoffed as he read the summons. Stephanie, his wife of two years, wanted out. No big deal. He'd use the same attorney as last time. Let her keep the house. He'd buy another with nothing down on the GI Bill. All he cared about was his pension, the marijuana he could steal from the evidence room, always in small amounts to avoid detection, his stereo gear and Delilah. Even though she had a kid, her legal and illegal lines of work turned him on.

CHAPTER THIRTEEN
Hitchcock's Ring of Spies

DESPERATE TO INTERCEPT the heroin Smith would be selling to kids, Hitchcock headed for the parks in Eastgate and Lake Hills in his El Camino as soon as he went off duty. He had no radio, no way to communicate with the station if he found Smith, but he couldn't rest without trying to catch him before he sold all the heroin.

He hunted the parks, school and bar parking lots for Smith's green Firebird. No luck.

Charlie's Place wasn't open yet. Wally Evans, the owner, was in his office, doing his books behind his massive wood desk, which was positioned out of place in an opposite corner of where one would expect. It was a simple security tactic to give Wally precious seconds to arm himself in the event of an armed intrusion.

Wally's face lit up when he saw Hitchcock.

"Well, well, if it isn't our young Romeo himself. Happy New Year, Roger. How are all your women treatin' ya?"

He shrugged. "Can't complain, I guess."

"Hah! The best-looking women in town are falling all over you," Wally chuckled, "and all you can say is 'can't complain.' Have a seat and tell me what brings the young heart-throb here off duty."

Hitchcock cracked a smile as he said, "First off, I'm trying to nail a guy who's hanging around parks like Robinswood peddling heroin to kids. Some of it is the black tar variety from Vietnam. We had two people die from it last year."

Wally scowled as he leaned forward on his desk. "As a parent, I want to know about this," he said. "If he comes in here, it'd be standard routine for us to ID him and anyone with him before we serve them. We'll give the details to you. Who is he?"

"Name's Mike Smith. White male, tall, thin, long blond hair, acne scars, drives a newer green Firebird with the hood emblem. He's twenty-one, so he might come in here. If he does, it's to peddle heroin or cocaine too, maybe. Call the station, tell them to call me asap. Tomorrow I'll show you his mugshot."

"Consider it done. What's the other thing you want to talk about?"

"You."

"Me?"

"I had no idea you did hard time until the detectives told me until after Wilcox was found murdered. Since whoever hired him to hit your place is still unknown, and I'm the one who foiled their plans, I need to be better informed."

Wally leaned back in his chair. His eyes narrowed to slits as they focused on Hitchcock. "What I tell you stays with you?"

"Absolutely."

Wally heaved his bulk out of his chair with a grunt, shut his office door and returned, resting his huge hairy forearms on his desk. Hitchcock wondered if Wally would mention the mysterious disappearance of his partner, Tony Adragna.

"I grew up in Chicago. Always in and out of trouble," Wally began. "Nothing serious, strictly smalltime stuff—shoplifting, dice, drinking underage, a few minor scuffles. I became friends with a guy in the neighborhood named Tony—Tony Adragna. He was a couple years older than me. We were quite the team; me, the mick, and Tony, the wop. A very unlikely duo in Chicago in those days, let me tell you," Wally said, smiling as he reminisced. "I defended Tony with my fists from my Irish pals, and Tony defended me from his Italian buddies in the same way."

"Then what happened?"

"I got drafted after I turned eighteen. Luckily for me, it was peacetime then. I was stationed in Germany. When I came home after my honorable discharge, Tony showed me the money he made running errands for mob guys. He took me in as a partner. We were errand and messenger boys for gambling, hookers and off-track betting operations that were run by, let's say *well-known* people. That's how I learned business—at O.J.T. University."

"What's O.J.T.?"

"On the Job Training. Chicago style."

"What brought you out here?"

"In '65 the Feds nailed me and Tony for laundering mob money. They offered us deals if we'd rat on those above us. We had wives, little kids, and homes, but we refused, knowing we'd go to prison."

"Then what happened?"

"We did our time at Joliet," Wally replied with a shrug. "Our bosses took care of our families' financial needs during our absence, and rewarded our loyalty with 'going away' cash when we got out. Tony and I pooled our money to come out here with our families. We bought this place and started over."

"What happened to Tony?"

"I'm coming to that. My wife faithfully waited for me, but Tony found out his wife got romantically involved with one of our bosses' enforcers while he sat in the can. I tried to talk him out of it, but Tony returned to Chicago to get revenge."

"This sounds like a movie script," Hitchcock said.

Wally cracked a quick grin as he went on. "When Tony couldn't find the guy, he snitched him off to the Feds. Arrests were made. Someone in the Feds leaked who it was, and Tony disappeared. He's probably wearing cement shoes in a lake or a river somewhere. He'll never be found."

"Why didn't you tell the detectives this when they talked to you about Wilcox?"

"Uhh, gee, Roger, I dunno. Cement shoes aren't my style. They fit snug enough, but there's something about 'em. Must be the weight."

"All right, dumb question. But you sure fooled me, Wally. You always seemed so upright."

Wally smiled proudly. "Oh, that's my wife Barbara's influence," he said. "I married up, to a 'good' girl. She wouldn't let me sleep with her until we were married, if you can imagine that in this day and age."

"I've been seeing someone like that."

"If she's good-looking, keep her."

Hitchcock chuckled as he thought of Allie. "Believe me—she is."

"I'm convinced the reason our marriage became so strong right away and still is, was because we waited," Wally said.

"Hmm," Hitchcock acknowledged with a slight nod.

"Barbara got religion, the born-again thing while I did my time in the joint. She says it made it easier to remain faithful to me. She prays for me a lot, and I go to church with her and the kids to set an example."

"You didn't trust the detectives enough to tell them about yourself, or your friend Tony, but you told me, a cop. Why?"

Wally pointed a thick finger at Hitchcock. "Because *you* saved my life and the lives of my friends and customers last fall, not them. The way *you* removed Wilcox from here, your gun under his chin, hammer cocked, was a scene right out of the movies. It convinced me that you're one of the few badges who really care about us. It made true believers out of my customers who saw the whole thing. They still talk about it."

"We still don't know who sent Wilcox here, or why, Wally."

Ignoring Hitchcock's remark, Wally continued. "As it was happening, I could tell you've killed before, probably in Vietnam, and I could tell Wilcox was picking up the same vibes—that you wouldn't hesitate to pull the trigger and you'd lose no sleep over it if you did. Though you're a kid, you're here for the benefit of *us*. Your heart's in your work. I also figured you came from good parents."

"Right on all counts," Hitchcock said.

"And when I read about you in the papers last year, one of the articles mentioned your late father was the town doctor here and coached Little League, I knew I figured it right."

"Thanks for the trust, Wally."

"Because I trust you, Roger, I want to tell you something important."

"What's that?"

"The way Wilcox operated and got bumped off isn't characteristic of any U.S. mob I know of. Whoever hired him and shut him up for good is new here, Russian or Oriental. You foiled their plans this time, but they're here and they're not going away."

"Noted," Hitchcock remarked.

Wally paused, looking Hitchcock in the eye. "The old saying 'one hand washes the other' is how I live. I won't take money for it, but I can tell you a lot about what goes on around here, behind the scenes and below the belts, too. Thanks to you I went home to my family that night. Thanks to you I'm protected, and what's mine is safer if I keep you informed. However..." Wally leaned an elbow on his desk and pointed a thick finger at Hitchcock. "*You* are the only badge I'll talk to."

"Thanks again, Wally."

"And, to show you I'm on the up-and-up, there is someone new here who needs your attention. She's been coming in here since the holidays, selling cocaine and something called 'angel dust' to my customers."

"You've seen this yourself?"

"So far, no. I've seen her here once, but Debbie, our barmaid and a couple of my regulars told me she's dealing."

"Who is she?"

"Name's Gina. A tough chick from out of state. Likes men, if you catch my drift. Works at Albertsons on the other side of the freeway as a meat cutter."

"Gina—Albertson's meat cutter," Hitchcock said as he wrote the information in his pocket notebook.

"I'm known around here for looking the other way when a few of the local divorced moms do a little weekend 'business' in their cars or the two motels across the driveway to keep their kids in shoes because hubby's gone, got laid off or is a deadbeat. But I won't tolerate dope trafficking or indecent behavior in my place. This is a clean, blue-collar, neighborhood bar."

"Got any more of Gina's description?"

"You'll know her you see her—she's the type that stands out in a crowd. Short and chunky, but not fat, early twenties, neck length, strawberry-blonde hair. Pretty face, a tattoo of a bracelet on her right wrist. Cusses like a sailor."

"What does she drive?"

"No clue."

"Use the code name 'Tony' when leaving messages for me at the station. They know how to find me off duty."

† † †

THE WAGON WHEEL was his next stop. The lounge was empty except for two couples in a booth and a man in overalls sitting at the bar. He slid into a corner booth with a view of the window and the entrance.

Gayle approached. "Hello, stranger," she said, pouting in her voice, looking photogenic in a black knee-length skirt, a crisp, long sleeved white blouse set off her ivory complexion, dark hair and eyes. He could believe her story that she modeled for Tacoma department stores before Rulee the drug pusher entered the picture. *Fashion model material still.*

She wasn't a happy camper.

"I'm working days now," he explained as she

poured his coffee.

"You're on mornings, four to noon, Tuesday and Wednesday off, to be precise. So, is rotating to day shift really the reason you don't come around anymore?"

Her knowledge of his schedule startled him. *Word travels fast in Eastgate! Who is she getting this information from?*

"Cut me a little slack. It takes a few days to adjust to the new hours. I'm getting up when you're asleep."

"Good. So now we can be together on afternoons again," she said, holding the coffee pot. She wasn't smiling.

Sultry, alluring, and streetwise described Gayle. Because of her dark past, she had a victim's perspective of society's underbelly that few people ever know. She escaped that part of her history, including drug addiction, on her own strength and fled Tacoma to Bellevue.

Later on, she became Hitchcock's informant. She wasn't in it for the money, but for Hitchcock himself. Knowing this, and that he was playing with fire, Hitchcock took a gamble that paid off with arrests, seized record amounts of hard drugs and took bad people off the streets. Some went to prison for the first time, several were returned to finish their time, two died violent deaths. But time was running out. He knew if she didn't get what she really wanted, she'd quit.

In the movies, James Bond never hesitated to get involved with beautiful women "for the Crown." In real life, romantic involvement with an informant, let alone a former junkie and hooker is a sure path to loss of credibility and badge.

So far, he hadn't crossed the line. Sergeant Baxter's warnings on his first night on duty rang in his ears every time he thought about going all in with Gayle: *"You'll meet women on this job who will throw themselves at you, and among them will be those who will compromise you for their own advantages. It'll seem innocent, even right, at first."*

It didn't take a degree in rocket science to know the more time he spent with Gayle, the more likely he was to succumb to her. She stood in front of him now, one hand on her hip, radiating sensual desire, frustration in her dark eyes.

"Tell Whitey I want the ribeye, medium rare, two eggs over medium, fruit cup, no toast or spuds," he said, changing the subject to buy time.

When she returned with his order, he told her about Mike Smith and the girl named Gina. As he forked a hunk of rib eye from his plate, Gayle surprised him.

"The Smith guy I don't know about, but Gina comes in here almost every day for drinks and dinner. Cuts meat at Albertsons, right?"

His fork stopped mid-air. "Tell me."

"Oops, new customers just came in. Excuse me." She left to greet them and came back only to hand him his bill. The note on the back read: GET BACK TO ME LATER ABOUT IT.

† † †

84

INSIDE CITY HALL that night, Deputy City Prosecutor Eve Claussen worked alone in her third-floor office, preparing for jury selection and opening arguments in the morning. She left the front door of the City Attorney offices open for Koji the janitor and his wife. A gentle, friendly couple, immigrants from Japan, in their late fifties who spoke broken English. Eve loved chatting with them and learning about Japanese culture.

Koji pushed his cart through the door to the offices of the attorneys. Unlike other times, he left the door to the City Manager's office open and the lights on when he finished.

"Hello, Koji. No wife with you tonight?"

Koji smiled and bowed to show respect in the tradition of his country. "Akimi sick with cold."

"Oh, I am sorry. Please tell her I hope she gets well soon."

Koji bowed again and pushed his cart to the back offices where he began cleaning.

Seizing a rare opportunity, Eve hurried into the offices of those who controlled the city. She saw a memo from Lieutenant Bostwick on the desk of the most junior assistant. What she read infuriated her. She hurried across the hall to the copy machine, returned the original and re-entered her office just as Koji came around the corner.

She hid her copies of the secret memo out of sight in her briefcase and closed the lid just in time. "I'm going home now, Koji," she said. "Tell your wife I said hello and that I wish her well."

† † †

EVE DOUBLE-LOCKED her apartment door, kicked off her shoes, and flopped upon her bed, meditating on her situation. *The risks are getting higher and there is more to do. Maybe I should stop.*

She thought about her mother's suffering after the town elites killed her father long ago. Even after she passed the bar exam, her credentials as an attorney couldn't move the state attorney general or the FBI to investigate her father's murder.

Hitchcock was a reincarnation of her father in many ways. Her father left college to join the Army and fight in World War II. He became a police officer when he came home instead of returning to law school. Hitchcock left medical school for the same reasons. She loved him in her own way, but put no strings on him. He had never said how he felt about her.

She didn't expect permanence in their relationship. She knew she wasn't the right one for him. For her there was no "right" one. But until the right one for Hitchcock comes along, she would enjoy intimacy with him. It wasn't their nine-year age difference. It was her—she wanted neither marriage, nor children, nor ties to any one man. For her, there are many men out there.

CHAPTER FOURTEEN
A Fall from Grace

Thursday - 3:45 A.M.
Shift Briefing

SERGEANT MARTIN CONRAD filled in again for Sergeant Breen on his days off. He kept district assignments the same except that he switched Hitchcock to downtown and put Clive Brooks in Eastgate. The men exchanged suspicious glances, sensing something was up, but no one commented.

At 4:32 a.m. Sergeant Conrad left the station in the marked supervisor's car, unannounced. He was heading for Crossroads when Hitchcock came on the air: "One Zero One, Radio, request Four Twenty contact me on F2."

Conrad switched to F2. *"Four Twenty to One Zero One, go ahead."*

"Found a commercial grade safe, about six feet tall,

in the open field south side of the Holiday Inn. Door's been forced open. It's empty. Fresh footprints and tire tracks indicate it was dumped here within the last hour – probably stolen from a downtown business. The prints and tracks won't last once it starts raining again."

Why does Hitchcock always have to be the eager beaver? Conrad keyed his mic again: *I'll tell Dispatch to call the detective sergeant and ask him what he wants to do.*

Disgusted, Hitchcock replied, "There's no time to wait for the dicks. I'm making casts of the footprints and tire tracks and processing the safe for prints before it rains. The safe weighs several hundred pounds. It will take a tow truck to move it. Send me a tow."

He popped the trunk and was reaching for plaster-of-Paris kit when he heard Conrad's reply: *"Find another unit to help you."*

Hitchcock cursed Conrad under his breath as he went to work.

He could tell it would rain any minute. Under his headlights on high beam, he assembled wood frames around the tire tracks and footprints, whipped up a batter of Plaster of Paris and distilled water which he poured into the frames.

Ray Packard, the District Two unit, arrived unannounced. Without a word he began photographing the scene and processing the safe for latent prints while Hitchcock worked on plaster casts.

The tow truck took almost an hour getting to the scene. Hitchcock's hands were numb from the cold as he placed the casts and Packard's latent print lifts in the trunk of his cruiser.

The rain finally let loose, drenching Hitchcock, Packard and the tow truck driver. They sloshed in the downpour, laboring with heavy chains plus block and tackle to suspend the safe in the air for the short drive to the station. They grunted, cursed and moaned as they struggled to tilt the safe enough to slip a heavy-duty hand-truck under it. They wrestled it up the stairs, down the hall and into the evidence room.

Wet, muddy and exasperated, Hitchcock poked his head in the dispatch center. "Anybody heard from Conrad?" he asked. All said they had not.

"Try to raise him on the air."

Radio to Four Twenty?

Dispatch tried again. *Radio to Four Twenty?*

No answer.

Otis came on the air: *"Someone please find him and put a blanket on him, so he doesn't catch a chill!"*

Others cracked jokes at Conrad's expense.

Conrad was still missing an hour later. A sense of emergency replaced the jokes. Traffic Division units coming on duty joined Patrol in the search for him.

RUSH HOUR CAME. Commuters in cars and buses filled the streets and the floating bridges across Lake Washington, heading for Seattle. Captain Delstra arrived at the station. The Dispatch supervisor knocked at his office door. "Captain, Sergeant Conrad, the duty sergeant, has been missing for almost four hours since he left in his patrol car."

Fearing the worst, that a cop had been in an accident or assaulted or assassinated, Delstra directed Patrol units to check the city gas pumps, the photo lab, and other city facilities. All assigned units reported negative results.

Records transferred a call to Delstra's office. The caller sounded nervous. "Uhh, I'm Joe Collier, Captain, just a regular citizen, don't wanna cause nobody no trouble, unnerstan'?"

"Okay, Mr. Collier, what can I do for you?" Delstra asked impatiently.

"Well, sir, uhh, a black an' white police car's been parked here, for hours, see? There ain't no overhead red light on the top, but I, uh, well, I peeked inside, an' nothin' there—"

Delstra shot out of his chair, clutching the phone. "Where *are* you Mr. Collier?"

"Uh, Villa La Paz apartments, n-north side."

Delstra thanked the caller, slammed the phone down and called Dispatch. "Delstra here. I need Otis on the line right away."

"We just sent him to a commercial burglary, Captain."

"Send another unit instead. Tell Otis to go to a pay phone and radio in the number now!"

Three minutes later Delstra called the phone booth

where Otis waited. "Joel, meet me at the east end of the Villa La Paz. Stay off the air."

"Come with me," Delstra ordered the station officer.

DELSTRA SPOTTED THE patrol supervisor's car in the north parking lot, facing the apartment building. It was unoccupied. The hood felt cold to the touch. Leaving the station officer to guard their vehicles, he took Otis with him into the building.

Sergeant Conrad emerged minutes later, fear in his eyes, mouth open, Otis escorting him by the arm, Captain Delstra following. Delstra seized Conrad's service revolver and set him in the back seat of Otis's cruiser.

At the station, Delstra's raised voice and Conrad's pleading erupted from Delstra's office. Minutes later the station sergeant led Conrad out of Delstra's office by the arm, minus his badge and gun belt. The epaulets of his uniform shirt had been torn off.

Across the hall, Lieutenant Bostwick left his office door open to overhear as much as he could. His cold hands trembled, his heart pounded, he stared at the papers on his desk as Conrad paused at his office door, trying to make eye contact with him. Bostwick didn't look up. "Move it, Conrad," the station sergeant ordered as he shoved Conrad from behind.

† † †

AT 9:00 A.M. the next morning, Martin Conrad appeared at Chief Carter's office on the second floor, where he met the Chief and Captain Delstra. Minutes later the desk sergeant escorted Conrad to the locker room to remove his things. Nine years up in smoke.

Hitchcock passed Conrad in the hallway as the duty sergeant led him to the door. Conrad stopped, his eyes burning with hatred. "They're *coming* for *you,* golden boy," he hissed. The desk sergeant pushed him toward the station door.

Hitchcock grabbed Conrad by his sleeve. "What do you mean by that?"

"You'll find out," Conrad snarled as he shook his arm free.

"Stand down, Roger," the station sergeant ordered as he forcefully led Conrad out of the building, leaving Hitchcock standing in the hallway, shaken.

CHAPTER FIFTEEN
Targeting the Pushers

THE CLOCK WAS ticking. Rumors and sightings of Mike Smith and his followers kept coming in from parents, teachers, bar tenders. The Patrol Division was all the Department had to respond to it. Hampered by having to handle calls and driving marked cars, they were always too late to catch anyone, and the city suffered.

Local drug dealers were taking advantage of Bellevue not having a narcotics unit. Overdose cases doubled in a month. The first cases were less than a week after former Sergeant Conrad failed to release Hitchcock's report about Mike Smith having a large shipment of heroin.

Frustrated by the administration's bumbling in a crisis, Hitchcock defied orders by going upstairs to Records after shift briefing before he hit the streets.

Smith's latest arrests with Bellevue were three years ago. The booking sheets showed the same address in

Carnation, a small town in the Snoqualmie Valley. Without asking anyone's permission, Hitchcock wrote up an information bulletin which included Smith's mug shot. Without prior approval he posted copies in the Patrol, Detective and Traffic briefing rooms and kept copies to release in the field.

Until he could visit Smith's last known address in Carnation, he would focus on identifying Gina, the alleged drug dealer who works at Eastgate Albertsons.

† † †

AFTER SHIFT BRIEFING, he took a portable radio with him as he left the station. It was still dark when he left his cruiser in front of the church above Albertsons and slipped through tall scotch broom brush to his position above the employee parking lot. It was cold but not wet or raining.

Two minutes later, he saw a white Camaro take the Highway 10 off-ramp and cross the overpass. It entered the Albertsons employee parking lot. Hitchcock focused his binoculars on the driver. It was the same woman.

Dispatch ended the silence. *"One Zero Six and One Zero Eight, silent alarm at Eastgate Safeway. Code Two."*

Hitchcock cursed as he acknowledged the call and crept back to his cruiser. He sped across the overpass and shut down his lights as he idled between the Sunset Lanes bowling alley and the Safeway store. He saw the headlights of a car coming around the other end of Safeway. He shut off his headlights and waited, his cruiser partly hidden behind a huge dumpster. He rolled his window down a crack and radioed in his arrival.

A full-size American sedan stopped at the loading dock behind the store. The lights went out. He heard two doors open and shut. Two men left the car, climbed the steps to the dock and entered the store—the rear door had been opened already. *Early employees,* he assumed.

Hitchcock keyed his mic: "One Zero Six is behind Eastgate Safeway now. Two men arrived in a car a minute ago. The back door was already unlocked. They went inside. Requesting backup."

Before Dispatch acknowledged, Walker pulled up behind him, headlights off.

"One Zero Six, Radio, One Zero Eight has arrived," Hitchcock reported. "We're going in through the loading dock. Call the store."

"Gotta be employees," Hitchcock told Walker "One used a key to unlock the back. The guy with him didn't look around at all. Probably normal, but since we're here, let's check."

Walker nodded and shrugged. "Better safe than sorry."

Flashlights in hand, holsters unsnapped, they climbed the short ladder to the loading dock and walked through the open door. Further within the store, they heard a phone ringing nonstop.

They stopped at the sounds of two male voices conversing and of boxes being moved. Following the noise, they located the two men in the cold storage area. The phone kept ringing.

"Show us some ID, boys," Walker ordered.

Both men were clean-cut types in their late twenties to early thirties. Each handed his driver's license to Walker. "We came early to make room for a new shipment of produce coming in later this morning, officer," one of them explained.

"We're here because you set off the silent alarm when you opened the door," Hitchcock said. "How come you guys didn't answer the phone?"

"We don't have a key to the office," the older of the two replied.

A stout, balding man in his thirties with a Safeway name tag on his white dress shirt walked through the loading door.

"Any trouble, officers? I'm Scott Dawson, the manager. These two fellas are my employees."

"We're here on a silent alarm, Mr. Dawson," Hitchcock said. "We tried to call the store, but your employees told us they have no access to the alarm or the phone. That aspect of your policy needs to be changed."

"Consider it done, Officer Hitchcock. Anything else?"

"The first employees to arrive should also know how to turn the alarm off when they enter, and call us," he advised.

Dawson smiled as he extended his hand to both

officers. "I appreciate your diligence. I'll make sure these changes are made right away."

† † †

AFRAID THAT HE might miss Gina's arrival at Albertsons, Hitchcock ran to his cruiser and sped across the freeway overpass and swung through the Albertsons parking lot. The white Camaro was unoccupied. The false alarm caused him to miss her arrival again.

He parked under the canopy of the A&W Root Beer drive-in a few yards from Albertsons and got out his binoculars. He radioed the plate number of the Camaro to Records. It came back to a '68 Camaro owned by Angelo Lucci, Issaquah address, no warrants. On a hunch that this might be Gina's last name, he asked Records to search statewide for Gina Lucci. No results.

Frustrated, he crossed back across the overpass and headed toward Art's.

† † †

A BROODING TENSION permeated the breakfast crowd at Art's when Hitchcock and Walker came through the door. The customers were unusually quiet and somber. No one made eye contact with either of them. In case they had walked in on a robbery in progress, they casually scanned the customers and checked the men's' restroom before they ordered their breakfast at the counter. They took their coffees to the only open table in the back.

Even Judy looked distraught as she took their orders.

"Everybody seems uptight this morning, even you, Judy. Something wrong?" Hitchcock asked.

"Where the hell have you been, Roger?" Judy shouted, fighting tears. "Damned Congress voted down the SST! People Boeing laid off last year still can't find work! They lost their homes and cars to the bank! Now, *more* folks are gonna get canned."

"It's bad all around," Walker sympathized.

Judy set her coffee pot on the table, put her hands on her hips as she faced them. "You boys better be grateful you got job security," she exclaimed. "We'll lose our home if Ross gets the axe this time!"

"We sure hope that doesn't happen to you and Ross," Walker sympathized.

Wiping tears from her eyes, Judy said, "With three kids still at home and one in college, and Ross near retirement, we could lose everything."

† † †

"I'M SURPRISED YOU didn't know about the Boeing layoffs, Roger," Walker said as they left Art's.

"I did know. Boeing is reducing its workforce from 103,000 to 39,000 in stages. Our unemployment rate is the highest in the nation."

"Then why did you act like you didn't know when Judy told you?"

"Oh—that," he smiled. "I was surprised when Judy

mentioned a husband. The way she carries on with Art, I thought he was her husband."

Walker bobbed his head slightly as he grinned. "To some folks, friendships matter more than anything."

"You mean, Judy's got two husbands?"

Walker nodded. "It's a longstanding arrangement, mutual in nature, and highly unusual," was his cryptic reply.

He stared at Walker, dismayed. "You mean all three know and agree to it? How—"

"Read the O. Henry story called '*Telemachus, Friend,*' to get a grip on it. It's a lot like Judy's arrangement," Walker cut in as he checked his watch. "It's six already. Let's get back to work."

† † †

TWO HOURS LATER he crept through thick scotch broom brush to the edge of the bank overlooking the employee entrance of the Albertson store and the parking lot.

He waited.

A woman matching Wally's description of Gina stepped outside the employee entrance. Three men were with her. Two of them held steaming paper coffee cups. they lit up cigarettes and talked, shivering in the cold.

The woman led the third man to the white Camaro.

The second Hitchcock put his binoculars on her, the name Jezebel came to mind. Jezebel of the Bible— murderous and manipulative, queen to King Ahab, whom she dominated as she did everyone around her.

Wally's description of her was spot-on, he thought as he studied her. Mid-twenties, chunky but shapely in a strong, sensuous way. Neck-length reddish hair. Feminine and fierce. A tattoo of a bracelet on her left wrist. An attractive face, high cheekbones, full, seductive lips, she was hard as a chisel. Her bloody hands, white shirt and meat-cutter's apron gave her a grisly, primeval sensuality that aroused the basest instincts of men.

She radiated evil.

The two smokers went inside. Gina and the other man got into the white Camaro, she in the driver's seat. Hitchcock could barely see into the interior due to the tinted glass. After a few minutes they exited the Camaro. He noted that even her walk bore the stamp of a predator.

CHAPTER SIXTEEN
A Dark Foreboding

THE RADIO CRACKLED as Otis came on the air over a man cursing in the background. *"One Zero Seven en route to the station with a felony prisoner. Request the station detail to meet me in the loading port. Got a fighter on board."*

Seconds later another man's voice was heard in the background cursing and yelling as Walker reported he too was headed to the station with a combative subject in custody.

Dispatch ordered Hitchcock to cover Crossroads and Lake Hills until Otis and Walker were clear. *A brief change of scenery will be welcome,* he thought as he headed north.

Sergeant Bill Harris pulled up to on his black-and-white Harley Davidson as Hitchcock finished a traffic stop.

"Let's grab a cup at Speed's," Harris said, pointing to the Greek style diner in the Lake Hills Shopping Center.

WHEREAS ART'S WAS a breakfast and lunch spot frequented by long-haul truckers, mechanics, highway road crews, and beat cops, Speed's was a working-class family style eatery, open for breakfast lunch and dinner.

Seven red round barstools affixed to the floor faced a pearl Formica counter. Booths and brown vinyl bench seats long enough to serve six adults lined both walls.

Except for four men in overalls wolfing down breakfast at the counter and the owner and his wife prepping food for the lunch crowd, the place was empty and quiet.

Hitchcock removed his hat and Harris his helmet as they settled into a booth with a window facing the parking lot. The waitress, a handsome, swarthy, thirtyish woman, gave Harris a lusty once-over from his gleaming riding boots to his sergeant stripes as she poured coffee for them and left.

"Like the other older guys on the Department," Harris began, flashing his signature smile. "I followed your Golden Gloves and Olympic careers. We were your biggest fans, and several of us were your dad's patients. So, I'm wondering if you would help out at the Boys Club."

"How?"

"By giving boxing lessons to boys in their early teens. Most of them come from permissive parents and dads who are seldom home. They're starving for structure, male coaching and discipline. The club's equipment is antiquated and basic: a ring, a couple heavy bags, and a speed bag."

When Hitchcock hesitated, Harris added, "I teach judo there to a class of seven thirteen-year-old boys once a week. They learn self-respect, respect for others and self-confidence. I'm reaching the next generation with values. I'm asking you to do the same on Saturdays with what you know."

Hitchcock sighed, looking at Harris. "You're gonna hornswoggle me into saying yes whether I want to or not, so my answer is sure, it's a great idea."

Harris nodded as he handed Hitchcock a folded piece of paper from his shirt pocket. "I knew you'd accept. Here's the manager's name and phone number. I told him you'd be calling. Thanks for helping the kids."

He resumed patrol in mostly empty neighborhoods, pondering the strange, expectant quiet. A major event was ahead, a shift. He could feel it.

Otis and Walker radioed they were back in service. He returned to Eastgate Albertsons. Gina's white Camaro was parked in a different space, indicating she went somewhere on her lunch break. Another opportunity to develop intel on her and her associates was lost.

Crossing back over the freeway, he spotted Wally's Oldsmobile station wagon parked in front of Charlie's Place. The janitorial crew was leaving as he walked in. Even empty and clean, the place smelled like beer, cigarettes and fried food. He found Wally leaning over papers and file folders piled on his desk.

Wally glanced up. "Hey, Roger."

"Got a minute?"

Wally sighed as he stood up. "Yep. I could use a break from number crunching. Let's step outside."

He showed Smith's mug shot to Wally. "This is the Mike Smith guy I told you about, reportedly selling heroin in the parks."

Wally studied the photo. "That's the guy, but he hasn't been here since we talked."

"If he shows up, see what he does and who he's with. He did time as a juvenile. He's got an adult felony rap sheet. The prosecutors downtown want him arrested for investigation homicide."

"What do you want me to do?"

"Since he is twenty-one, check his ID and anyone with him. Memorize or write down their names, dates of birth and addresses. Try to small-talk Smith. Better yet, ask Debbie. She'd be perfect. If possible, call me while Smith is here. If he leaves, call the number I gave you, use your code name. I'll call you back to find out what was learned, if anything."

Wally nodded with grim finality. "You bet. If he comes in, we'll hold him for ya."

† † †

HE AVOIDED THE Wagon Wheel. Neither Gayle nor Ralph were there this early and he knew no one else there well enough to trust with sensitive information.

He checked his watch: Time to refuel and turn in.

Dispatch came on the air: *"Radio to One Zero Eight."*

"One Zero Eight," Walker replied.

"Respond Code One to a D.O.A. 18259 SE Tenth Place. Apparent drug overdose. Ambulance attendants are standing by. A detective unit is leaving the station and will meet you there."

As Walker acknowledged the call, Hitchcock hung a U-turn.

CHAPTER SEVENTEEN
The Dead Girl Mystery

HE SAW WALKER'S cruiser in the driveway of a small, light green, late '50s starter home. A robin's egg blue mid-'60s Buick Special sedan sat in an attached single car carport. A Plymouth Belvedere sedan was parked on the street in front of the house. Two uniformed attendants from the new Bellevue Ambulance Service waited across the street, arms folded, leaning against a white Dodge commercial van with blue markings.

"Hang tight, I'll be right back," Hitchcock asked them. He went inside.

The front door opened right into the living room. A thick green shag carpet covered the floor. The walls were taupe-colored, and the ceiling was the white popcorn stuff they spray on to deaden echoes in the room. What he could see of the house was neat, everything in its place and it smelled clean.

A petite, attractive woman in her late thirties, dressed in a brown pinstriped ladies' business suit, ivory colored silk blouse. She was brunette. Her hair was coiffed neatly in a bouffant hairdo just below her ears. She sobbed uncontrollably on the living room couch, her face buried in her hands. The only words Hitchcock could make out were "my baby, my baby, I'm so sorry..." A putty-faced, overweight, fiftyish Catholic priest sat next to her, one hand on her shoulder, doing his best to console her.

The clean smell in the living room changed to one Hitchcock was familiar with as Walker led him down the hall. In a small bedroom at the end, the body of a teenage girl laid supine on a single bed pushed up against the wall. A poster of John Lennon and a black-and-white scene of the Woodstock festival were thumb-tacked to the wall.

She was taller than her mother, slim and pretty, long straight dark brown hair and bangs like Cher the rock singer. She wore a string of love beads around her neck, bell-bottom blue jeans, large collared white shirt, her brown suede vest had a peace symbol pin on the front. Her eyes were dead, unseeing slits. Her lips were parted slightly as if in a stupor.

"The body's been moved," Hitchcock said as he examined the purplish blotches of advanced postmortem lividity on right side of her face and neck. The left side was ashen and waxy.

"Yeah. Hours after death," Walker added.

Hitchcock lifted her wrist. "Rigor is leaving. Time of death about midnight. Why the ambulance?"

"Strong denial on the mom's part, apparently," Walker replied, scowling. "She told me her daughter didn't come home from school until late last night. Said she doesn't know who she would have been with."

"Her shoes are still on, isn't that odd," Hitchcock observed. "Let's see what the back of her looks like."

They exchanged significant glances when they rolled the body onto the right side.

"Uh-oh.," Hitchcock scoffed. "Mom's got some 'splainin' to do," he said, looking at grass clippings and dirt in the back of the dead girl's hair and ground into her jacket.

"The body must've been on the lawn, maybe dumped there," Walker added. "Had to take two people to lug her into the house and set her on the bed. This blows Mom's explanation to bits."

"Umm-hmm. To smithereens. What *has* Mom said besides she came home late?"

"That she couldn't wake her daughter up this morning, so she called an ambulance. The ambulance crew told me they took one look at the body told her the police should be called. She not only refused to call us herself, but she also didn't want them calling us either. They went outside and had their dispatcher call us. They're waiting to give their statements."

"It's past noon," Hitchcock said. "We have evidence

the body was outdoors, that it's been moved indoors, the state of lividity and rigor indicate death occurred about six to eight hours ago."

"When the coroner takes the core body temperature, we'll have a better fix on the time of death," Walker said.

"From what we know now, there's about four hours of missing time," Hitchcock speculated.

"Looking more like murder by the minute," Walker muttered, staring at the dead girl.

"Want me to take the ambulance guys' statements so you can keep talking to the mom?"

"That would help, Roger. Also gather samples of the grass and dirt from the front lawn for comparison to the debris on the girl. The grass blades on her back are cut, like from a lawnmower. She was only fifteen, according to Mom," Walker said grimly.

"She has no *obvious* injuries, that I see."

"Her left cuff was unbuttoned, so I looked at her arm. Fresh tracks."

Hitchcock looked around the room. "It's too neat in here for a teenage doper. Where're the needles, baggies or bongs or pipes?"

"Someone did some tidying."

"Uh-huh, making sure we find nothing,"

"Remember to check the trash before we go."

"Do you think Mom is strong enough to move a dead body of this size from the front yard, all the way through the house, and set it on the bed?"

Walker shook his head. "Someone else is involved."

"I'll get statements from the ambulance guys so they can go, and collect samples from the front lawn."

† † †

"WE NEVER TOUCHED the body, officer," the taller attendant told Hitchcock. "She was beyond help."

"The mother was hysterical," the second attendant said. "She insisted we give her CPR. We refused, saying she was too far gone. When I said we had to call the police, she wouldn't let us use her phone."

"What else did she say?"

"She wanted Green's Funeral Home to pick the body up," the second attendant said as he folded his arms. "When she overheard us radio our dispatcher to call the police, she went nuts. Ordered us to go away, so we waited out here for you guys."

Hitchcock took notes on the small spiral notepad from his shirt pocket as he listened. "Did the mother say what happened?"

"Said her daughter didn't come home from school yesterday, then found her in bed like that in the morning," the first attendant said.

Totally different than what she told Walker. "What was the body position when you arrived?"

"Flat on her back on the bed, arms at her sides, like she was in a coffin."

"She was dressed like she had been outside. Even her shoes were on," the second attendant said.

Detectives Joe Small and Larry Meyn arrived.

111

Hitchcock interrupted his statement taking to go over the details with them.

"Thanks, Roger. We'll talk with the mom now."

Frank Kilmer the city photographer and the County Coroner's investigator arrived as the detectives entered the house.

After Kilmer finished, Hitchcock and Walker helped the coroner investigator use the bedsheet to transfer the body to the gurney, to hold the debris under the body for laboratory examination.

The mother descended into shrieking as the officers and the coroner's investigator rolled her daughter's body through the living room out of the house.

Hitchcock was troubled as he put on surgical gloves, clipped samples of the front lawn grass and took soil samples which he placed in evidence envelopes. He was troubled as he cleared the scene.

AFTER HE BOOKED the grass clippings and soil samples into evidence, Hitchcock went home. He fed Jamie and called the Pancake Corral to tell Allie he would be working for a couple more hours. He returned to the scene. Only the mother's Buick, the detective car and Walker's black-and-white remained.

The front door was slightly ajar. He crept close until he could hear the mother and the detectives talking. What began as an interview of a grieving parent had shifted into full interrogation mode.

"Okay, you admit you lied to us, Kate. That's a big step in the right direction, which was a brave step you took, Kate," Detective Meyn said.

The mother began hyperventilating and sobbing, taking short, loud breaths.

A long minute of silence ensued.

"You're feeling better now, aren't you, Kate?" the detective's voice suggested.

"Y-yes," the mother's voice said between sniffles.

"You're under a lot of stress, Kate. What happened is tearing you up, you don't know what to do, right?"

Kate said nothing. Meyn continued.

"Explaining *why* you lied and *why* you moved your daughter's body would take that stress off your shoulders Truth is the surest route to relief. Let's start again at the beginning and be honest this time."

"All right, all right—I lied..." she said, her words gushing forth like a waterfall. "Yes-yes, I moved her body. But I loved my little girl. She was all I had! Why would I do anything to hurt her?" she shrieked, her hysteria mounting between sobs.

"You're in over your head in this, Kate," Meyn persisted in a calm, fatherly tone. "You feel like the walls are coming at you. Your mind has locked up. You're waiting to wake up from a bad dream, this *can't* be real. Right, Kate?"

Kate made no reply.

"Right, Kate?" Meyn pursued.

"Yes," she said, in a hoarse whisper. "I feel

trapped."

"The only sure way out of the trap is the truth. It may hurt, Kate, but holding it in will destroy you and you don't want that, do you Kate?"

Kate said nothing.

"Do you, Kate?" Meyn pressed in.

"No," Kate whispered.

"Is it possible that you're protecting someone else in this, Kate?" Detective Meyn asked softly.

Kate sniffed. Meyn repeated the question.

"It's possible," she replied, her voice breaking.

"Tell me the person's name, Kate," Meyn persisted.

Kate stammered through her sobs. "Stacey—she-she had been s-seeing somebody named Mike, or Spike...or something. That's all I know!"

"'Mike or Spike'?" Detective Meyn echoed. "Outstanding, Kate!" he said in a congratulatory tone. "Now we're getting somewhere. Did Mike help you move Stacey's body, Kate?"

"I told you before, no one helped me."

"How tall are you, Kate?" Detective Meyn asked.

"Five-one."

"And how much do you weigh?"

"Ninety-five pounds. Why?"

"You're shorter and lighter than your daughter and you want us to believe you moved your daughter's body by yourself?"

Silence.

HITCHCOCK ALERTED TO the fact that once again, the parent of a dead or missing girl reported their daughter had been involved with a mysterious man with blond hair named Mike whom they had never met. He knew what to do next.

CHAPTER EIGHTEEN
The Mom Mystery

IT GRATIFIED HITCHCOCK to see Randy Fowler at the kitchen table, finishing a bowl of stew with biscuits. Gaunt and frail no longer, Randy's ruddy complexion had returned, and his eyes were clear when he looked at his friend. It also pleased him to see the house so clean and orderly, but he left those compliments at the door.

"You look much better than the last time I saw you."

"I feel better. Pull up a chair. Mom made fresh stew and biscuits," Randy said. "Connie, please get Roger a bowl and a biscuit."

"Thank you no, Connie. I'm here on business." He turned to Randy. "Anything new from Mike Smith?"

"He didn't show up like he said he would, but he called me at the station today—said he'll see me there tomorrow."

"For what?"

"Didn't say, but it's gotta be about the smack he showed me the other day. Said he needs a partner now that Guyon is dead, and business is growing. If he comes by, what should I do?"

"Listen to his offer, act like you're interested, ask questions like what's in it for you, tell him you'll get back to him in a day. Then call me."

"Okay, Roger. Anything else?"

"Do you know if Smith has or had a girlfriend?"

Randy thought for a second. "I saw a chick with him back then, but that was over a year ago. Why?"

"A fifteen-year-old girl died yesterday here in Lake Hills. Apparent heroin overdose."

Barbara gasped. "Oh, my!"

"Do you remember how Smith met girls?"

Randy lowered his head in thought for a few seconds. "Uh, Robinswood Park is all I saw."

"The dead girl's name is Stacey Brock. Lived near Robinswood Park. Anything you can find out will help. And next time Mike Smith comes around, write down the plate number of his car."

Randy's eyebrows lifted when he heard the name. "Stacey? Long hair, looks like Cher, hippie chick, kinda tall, skinny, eighth grade?"

"That's the one."

"She hung out after school and Friday nights at the old barn at Robinswood Park. Smoked weed a lot. Always there when I was. She would've known Smith."

"How often are we talking about?"

"Once a week, sometimes more."

He pressed further. "Did you ever know or hear of Stacey having contact with Tyrone Guyon?"

Randy thought for a second, then shook his head.

"Not that I ever saw or heard."

"Smith got you hooked on heroin," Hitchcock said, "then one day Tyron Guyon came over from Seattle and ran Smith off. So how did Guyon know about you as someone who was already addicted to heroin?"

Randy was perplexed. He looked at the floor, shaking his head, thinking. "Good question. I'd *like* to know but I don't even remember, it's such a blur."

"Okay," Hitchcock pressed on, "who do you know of that Stacey hung out with?"

"Girls her own age is all I ever saw," Randy replied with a shrug. "None of 'em had wheels. I never talked to her. I can find out more. Everybody'll be talking about what happened."

"Who were her closest friends?"

"Carla Jenkins and Naomi Tatum are the two I saw her with the most."

"If Stacey and her friends don't have wheels, how do they get the money to buy dope?"

"Carla's parents give her a weekly allowance, or so I hear."

"What about Stacey and Naomi?"

"Naomi steals money from her parents."

"And Stacey?"

Randy hesitated. His eyes flashed to his mother who

was busy tending to the stove. "Favors," he murmured.

"Okay. One more thing. When *you* got heroin from Smith, who did he get it from?"

"Some guy in Seattle, and someone else who owns a business in Eastgate. He never said which one."

"Names?"

"I never asked. Too stoned."

"Did he say if the business owner in Eastgate is a man, or a woman?" Hitchcock asked.

Randy paused, thinking. "It's a woman, I think."

Hitchcock suppressed the urge to grin, he believed he could fill in the blank with the correct answer. If only he had proof.

"Stay in touch, Randy." Barbara Fowler nodded her approval as he started through the door.

He stopped and went back inside. "I almost forgot— you're recovering from heroin addiction, so I don't want you exposing yourself to other users. Your family's gone through too much."

"How am I to help, then?"

"Just keep your eyes and ears open since you're in the community. Don't go out of your way to develop information. If Smith shows up tomorrow, call me right away. No James Bond stuff. Got it?"

"Got it."

† † †

HE WENT HOME and dialed Allie's new phone number. "Come over now," she said, "I'm getting hungry holding dinner for you."

How did she know I'd be over for dinner—or did I forget?
"Be there in ten," he said.

Allie opened the door before he could knock a third time. She pulled him inside by the arm and kissed him fully before he could say a word. The welcoming aromas of beef and vegetables simmering on the stove and bread fresh out of the oven filled the apartment. He hugged Trevor. Jamie sat where he could keep an eye on everybody and the door.

After dinner, Allie put Trevor to bed. Jamie repositioned himself at Trevor's bedroom door. Allie brought Turkish coffee and baklava for dessert to the couch. It had been an evening he didn't want to end. He wanted to stay longer, but three a.m. comes early.

† † †

THOUGHTS OF THE dead teenage girl went through his mind as he drove home. Stacy's mother, a young, attractive, office type, seemed too clean-cut, too 'normal' to even know about illegal drugs, let alone use them herself. That such an outwardly normal member of society would be involved in criminal conduct such as drugs was hard for him to accept. Before this he had thought of the drug realm involving only the fringe elements of society. This case opened his mind to an ugly truth: the tentacles of the drug culture were spreading upward.

The mother's well-groomed professionalism, her tidiness skewed his perception of her. If he read or heard her behavior without seeing her, his logical conclusion would be that she was either involved in or has guilty knowledge of her daughter's death. It would be enough to arrest her for investigation homicide on the spot.

A history of mental illness, or a state of extreme shock might explain her conflicting statements. But neither would explain her moving the body several hours after death. For that she had to have had help.

It was a messy case. Mulling over its many implications robbed him of precious hours of much-needed sleep. Three a.m. comes early.

CHAPTER NINETEEN
Slip-Sliding Away

Friday - 3:45 A.M.
Shift Briefing

"THE AUTOPSY OF yesterday's apparent overdose victim will be this morning," Sergeant Breen announced, his face somber. "The victim was a fifteen-year-old white female. She had needle marks on her left arm. The dicks arrested her mother for investigation of homicide. She's on suicide watch in the slammer."

The squad room was quiet. Breen turned to Walker. "Ira, you were there. Can you share anything more with us?"

Walker glanced around the room. "The short version is the mom told us three conflicting stories about how she found her daughter, and when and where she saw her last," he replied. "The dicks arrested her on the advice of the prosecutor after the third story turned out to be another lie. She admitted she moved the body and destroyed evidence before we got there. She told the dicks her daughter had been running around with some guy by the name of Mike, but she never met him. Looks like this could be the Mike Smith we've been looking for."

"Anything else?" Breen asked.

"We found drugs and drug paraphernalia in the outside trash bin," Walker replied. "Mom admitted it was in her daughter's room and she hid it from us."

† † †

IT WAS RAINING when Hitchcock and Walker met in front of Eastgate Safeway, car-to-car, before sunrise. Walker rolled his window down. Walker looked depressed. After a thoughtful pause he said: "I want to believe this is an accidental death, but the mother's behavior tells me otherwise. Someone else is involved, if only to help move the body to the bedroom. It's another homicide by overdose. It's hard to believe the girl's own mom is guilty, but either she is or knows who is."

Hitchcock nodded. "Death by overdose is Mike Smith's M.O. If we can prove Stacey ran with him, it would give us probable cause to arrest him. Learning the details of her relationship with Smith from her friends ought to help us find him."

"Girls talk. Stacey's bound to have told her friends about Smith. I know most of 'em and their parents. We'll find him," Walker said. "Anything else?"

"An informant told me Smith will be stopping by the Lake Hills Chevron sometime today. He always shows up in the late morning or early afternoon."

"I'll set up across the street in the Samena Club parking lot. What's he driving?"

"Green Firebird, new. Mag wheels. Hides baggies of heroin behind the driver side dash and in the console."

Walker nodded as he wrote in his notebook.

"The same informant told me Stacey hung out with Carla Jenkins and Naomi Tatum at Robinswood Park."

"Know 'em both," Walker said, "and their parents. Chronic runaways. Potheads, but likeable. They'll talk to me."

Hitchcock started his engine. "I'm going across the freeway to Albertsons to set up for Jezebel's arrival. Stay close to Eastgate for the next couple hours. I might need you in a hurry."

† † †

THE RAIN STOPPED. Hitchcock parked his black-and-white on the opposite side of the church above the back of the Albertsons store. He crept into the brush of the embankment above the Albertsons side parking lot. The cold ground and wet brush made for uncomfortable concealment, but the perfect view of the employee parking lot and the rear loading dock made up for it.

At 5:51 a.m. an older Ford pickup, occupied solely by a male driver arrived and parked in the employee parking lot. The driver didn't get out.

At 5:56 a.m., the white Camaro arrived, driven by the

same woman. A dark-haired man got out of the truck and walked over to the driver's side of the Camaro, hands in his front pockets.

He focused his binoculars through the Camaro windshield as the woman rolled down her window.

With a smirk on his face the man handed the woman something from his pants pocket. Hitchcock watched her count the money then count out a handful of plastic baggies from her shoulder bag and give them to the man. He put them in his jacket pocket and entered the rear employee entrance of Albertsons.

The woman he only knew as Gina locked the Camaro and entered the store the same way.

He ran the license number of the pickup when he returned to his cruiser. Renton address, no warrants on the registered owner. He updated his logbook, ending the latest entry with the notation: GINA'S LAST NAME STILL UNKNOWN.

No calls were holding when he radioed back in service.

† † †

AT 11:00 A.M. Walker was position in the empty parking lot of the Samena Club across Lake Hills Boulevard from the gas station, waiting for Mike Smith to show up. The distance from the gas station was about eighty yards. He had a clear view of Randy Fowler working on the lube rack.

The radio buzzed: *"Radio to One Zero Eight, respond to a completed suicide at 1520 156th SE. The Coroner's Office has been called. A detective unit will respond from the station."*

A middle-aged cowgirl type, no makeup, wearing jeans, plaid shirt with pearl-snap buttons, bleached hair in a ponytail, waved Walker into the driveway. The house, a late '50s, low-slung ranch-style one-story house set back from the road, was by itself, surrounded by the green bog it was built on.

Without a hint of emotion, she came up to Walker's cruiser and said, "The body's in the back."

"Lead the way, ma'am," Walker said, noting her detachment in referring to the decedent.

The body of a lean white male in his late forties laid supine in the middle of a rough concrete backyard patio, made long ago by someone with homeowner level skills. Between his legs and arms laid an antique .22 single-shot rifle, the barrel pointed at his head. Like the woman, he wore Western-style jeans, black cowboy boots and a denim shirt with pearl snap buttons. Blood had dried around the small bullet hole under his chin.

Walker reached down and tugged on the cuff of a pant leg. The entire body was stiff with rigor mortis. He turned to the woman.

"And you are...?"

"Annette Colville. That man there is—was—my husband, Tom."

"This is hard for you, but we need to understand what led up to this."

"Our marriage has been on the rocks for years. Tom

was in the first wave of Boeing layoffs last year. His unemployment ran out. The house goes back to the bank next week."

"He's been dead for over four hours," Walker noted as he studied the body.

"I moved out two weeks ago. I came over to check on him when he didn't answer the phone," she explained.

"You don't seem surprised by this, ma'am."

"Tom threatened to kill himself twice last year if he didn't find work," she said matter-of-factly.

"Did he leave a note or a message of any kind?"

"I only went into the house to call you guys."

"Did he have life insurance?"

She hesitated. Walker turned to make eye contact. "He did."

"And the beneficiary is...?"

"Our daughter, who just died of heroin overdose."

"So now the beneficiary is...?"

She hesitated again. "Me. I suppose you're thinking I did this, but you're wrong."

Detective Meyn entered the back yard. Walker took him aside to brief him before introducing him to the not-so-grieving widow. The coroner's investigator arrived and Walker hurried back to his surveillance post.

Using binoculars, he saw Randy Fowler working on the lube rack. After an hour, he concluded that if Smith had shown up, he missed it.

CHAPTER TWENTY
Morning Countdown

The Station
8:00 A.M.

LIEUTENANT BOSTWICK RECOGNIZED the writing on an envelope shoved under his office door. An evil grin spread across his face when he read the unsigned note inside. He dialed an extension on the third floor.

"Lieutenant Bostwick here. My inside man just informed me that the officers you are interested in, and many more are deliberately violating Department rules and regulations regarding ammunition. I'm going to catch them in the act at shift briefing today. It would behoove you to witness an event that will certainly be historic."

"Why should I be there?" The East Coast accent asked.

"The very presence of someone from your office when I catch officers engaged in illegal behavior will not only intimidate the officers," Bostwick said, a tone of conspiracy in his voice, "it will embarrass and weaken the Chief and Captain Delstra. Either they don't know officers are carrying unauthorized ammunition, or they know and allow it by their silence. Whichever is the case, they should be held accountable."

"Ah, I see. What time, then, *Bahstwick*?"

"Absolutely no later than 11:40. Half of the men my informant named are on duty now and will be coming in at noon, the other half will be having shift briefing at 11:45. I want to hit the ones at briefing first, while they're in the squad room, then I'll nail the men coming in from the morning shift," Bostwick said, power and malice in his voice.

"Getting approval shouldn't be a *prahblem*. I will be at your office at *eleven fahrty*."

"Bring a notebook so you can write down the names of the violating officers! Seeing someone from the city manager's office taking down names and questioning officers will scare anyone out of defending them in any way," Bostwick urged, almost unable to contain himself.

"I see. The old 'divide and conquer' idea, eh?"

"Precisely," Bostwick answered.

AT 10:00 A.M. Hitchcock resumed hiding in the brush above the Albertsons employee parking lot. Minutes later, the woman he believed to be Gina stepped outside with the same three male employees he had seen her with a day earlier. She and one of the men got into her

Camaro. With his binoculars he watched them light up what appeared to be marijuana cigarettes.

He fought the urge to swoop in and make an arrest. *A move like that now over a misdemeanor would ruin my chances to intercept the hard drugs. Better to wait.*

When Jezebel and the employees returned to work ten minutes later, he resumed patrol.

† † †

11:00 A.M.

IN A SECLUDED private residence one mile east of City Hall, the prowler who escaped from Hitchcock last October backed out of his garage in a late-model gun-metal gray Dodge Aspen. He special-ordered it with a 360 V-8 engine instead of the standard six-banger, and the performance suspension package. Its nondescript body style and neutral color were ideal for stalking victims, its power mill for outrunning the police. It wore Oregon plates to throw off the cops.

He headed for Lake Hills.

To his excitement the same VW Beetle driven by his next victim was parked in driveway of the same house he saw her enter a week ago. Learning the layout of a house, scouting the neighborhood and stalking the intended victim turned him on almost as much as the act itself.

He cruised the neighborhood, selecting two escape routes, one for normal departure, the other route in case the police arrived too quickly. He parked two blocks away and made a show of stretching his quadriceps and calves, then jogged in the direction of his next victim's house.

† † †

The Station
11:45 A.M.

AS LAPERLE HEADED down the hall from the booking room, he happened to see one of the interns to the city manager's office emerge into the hall from the stairwell. He was a skinny kid in a white short-sleeve dress shirt, brown bow tie, thick glasses, carrying a clipboard. He passed officers and clerks with an air of superiority about him, glancing at them as a teacher notices pupils between classes.

He left the door ajar when he entered Lieutenant Bostwick's office without knocking. LaPerle crept closer and listened.

"Okay, Lieutenant. What's next?"

"My source informs me the officers going on shift in a few minutes are all carrying unauthorized, hollow-point bullets, illegal ammunition, in their guns," Bostwick said, his voice bubbling with excitement. "I'm going to pull a surprise inspection of the ammunition in each gun and suspend or terminate each officer I catch with unauthorized ammunition!"

"How reliable is your information?"

"Oh-ho-ho, don't worry," he chortled. "My mole worked with these men and saw them regularly use this ammunition with his own eyes. He saw them loading it into their guns and talking about it in the locker room within the hour. Now is the time! We'll nail the ones in the squad room first, then the ones coming in from the morning shift, and bingo, the two officers you're after and others can be fired," Bostwick smugly assured him.

LaPerle hurried into the squad room. The afternoon shift sergeant, Lane Baxter, had not yet arrived.

"Quick, boys!" he urged, "Bostwick's on his way with one of the bow-tie squirrels from the third floor to inspect the ammo in our guns. I heard him say he would suspend or fire anyone caught with non-issue ammo."

The officers stood as one man, emptied their revolvers and reloaded with issue ammo from their dump pouches. They finished moments before Sergeant Baxter entered the squad room.

Lieutenant Bostwick strode into the squad room seconds later, looking as haughty as Hitler did when he conquered Paris, with the pencil-necked nerd following.

"Stand aside, sergeant, I'm taking over this briefing," Bostwick said with a dismissive wave of his hand.

Baxter's mouth fell open as Bostwick faced the men. "On your feet, every one of you."

"What's the meaning of this, Lieutenant?" Sergeant Baxter demanded angrily.

The men stood. Starting at the front row, Bostwick ordered one officer at a time to remove and show him the ammunition in his revolver.

LaPerle slipped outside and caught Otis as he arrived. "Someone told Bostwick a lot of our guys carry hollow-points in their weapons instead of the crap the Department issues. I warned 'em second shift just in time. Bostwick's coming out here next to catch us as we come in."

Otis stayed in the parking lot and warned every returning first-shift officer to switch back to standard issue ammo before entering the station.

After the last officer's gun passed inspection in the squad room, Bostwick turned to the young man from upstairs. His jowls shook as he tried twice to say something to the enraged young man whose face was purple, but no words came. "I-I don't know what to-to say," he finally managed to stammer.

Swallowing hard, his face crimson with bottled-up rage, the intern glared at Bostwick. "You have said too much already, *Bahstwick!* You have *damaged* us with this, *Bahstwick!* Be assured, *you* will face consequences."

SERGEANT BAXTER CONFRONTED Bostwick in the hallway. "Lieutenant! Unless you have a credible explanation for your unwarranted actions and violation of the rules regarding the chain of command, I'm filing a complaint against you."

Bostwick ignored him and stormed outside, followed by the intern.

The intern looked devastated. Bostwick's fumbling

had exposed the collaboration between Bostwick and his office, an enormous political setback for the people he worked for and himself. *Unless* Bostwick caught an officer, just one, with unauthorized ammunition, his career with Bellevue city management was over.

Outside the station door, he stopped and whirled on Bostwick. "You said your information is reliable, *Lieutenant*." He spit out Bostwick's rank as if something rotten was in his mouth.

"I can't explain it now, but we'll get the ones coming in. Please be patient," Bostwick replied, panic in his eyes.

Bostwick's face turned blood red after each of the returning first shift officers, including Hitchcock and Sherman, showed the ammunition in his weapon was issue ammo.

The intern violently shook his finger in Bostwick's face, grunting, unable to speak. He stomped back into the building.

Bostwick collapsed into his chair, numb, eyes unseeing, his mind wondering what happened and what would become of him since it was by his own stupidity that he exposed his schemes and his alliances upstairs.

He leaned forward to listen when he heard someone knock on Captain Delstra's office door across the hall.

"Erik, can I have a word with you? It's important." It was Sergeant Baxter.

"Sure, Lane, come on in," Captain Delstra replied.

Hearing that, Bostwick's heart sank.

LAPERLE CAUGHT UP with Hitchcock and Walker as they were heading toward their cars in the library parking lot. "I overheard Bostwick say he had an informant within the ranks who used to work with us," he told them.

Hitchcock glanced at Walker, who was staring at him, then they looked at LaPerle. None uttered the name. They knew who the Judas was.

CHAPTER TWENTY-ONE
The Reset

Friday - 12:45 P.M.
The Station

HITCHCOCK WATCHED AS Mark Forbes backed the Warrant Detail's black Ford Fairlane into the prisoner loading bay. His senior partner, Brendan O'Rourke exited the front seat and went inside with paperwork. Forbes opened the left rear door and man-handled a passive, roughed-up prisoner out of the back seat and marched him down the hall.

He followed Forbes and the prisoner to the booking room. "Hey, Mark, how's it going?"

Forbes, who liked Hitchcock, smiled. "Good. You?"

"I miss the action of nights, but I like the hours of days. What time are you off?"

"Right after this. What's up?"

"I'm teaching boxing classes at the Boys Club. The ring is empty for the next few hours. I thought if you're up for it, I can teach you what you need to know in one lesson, maybe two."

Forbes's face lit up at the offer. Hitchcock, a Golden Gloves champion and member of the '64 U.S. Olympic boxing team, saved him last fall from certain brain damage, or even death by the hands of Crawford Beecham, a modern-day outlaw. He remembered lying on the asphalt, wounded and helpless when Hitchcock crushed Beecham in seconds, using only his fists without receiving so much as a scratch to himself.

"Got my gym clothes in my car, Roger."

"Super. See you at the Boys' Club about one-thirty."

† † †

FORBES SPENT MUCH of his off-duty time building a fine physique. Three to four hours at a time, four times a week, he worked out at an upscale gym in downtown Bellevue. A hoity-toity place The Athena was. Mirror-covered walls, white plaster statues of gods and goddesses from Greek mythology and fake marble columns. There were machines designed to isolate and shape certain muscle groups, stationary bicycles and treadmills, dumbbells and barbells. A steam bath, sauna, ice-water dunking tub, and massage services occupied the far end.

Compared to Forbes's gym, the Bellevue Boys Club amounted to a third world country. It was old-school: sparse, well-worn equipment. The very air held a musty reminder of the sweat of earlier generations of young athletes.

A junior-size, three-rope boxing ring with frayed padding on the corner posts was tucked into one corner. Along one wall two heavy punching bags hung by chains from the ceiling over a worn wooden floor. Next to the heavy bags hung a wall-mounted speed bag. Wall-hooks held several skip-ropes. Cracked vinyl wrestling mats were stacked out of the way in another corner.

Out of gratitude to Hitchcock, Forbes refrained from snide remarks about the facility, though he felt the crude environment was beneath him. He came only for a chance to learn from Hitchcock, his personal hero.

The dressing room disappointed Forbes, but he changed into his gym shorts, tank top and gym shoes without comment. He put on a tank top shirt to impress Hitchcock with his rippling muscle mass.

Hitchcock was ready and waiting, wearing gray sweatpants and sweatshirt when Forbes came out of the dressing room. "First thing we do is warm up, Mark. We start with a different style of jumping jacks."

Starting at one wall, facing the room, Hitchcock demonstrated. "Leap forward about a foot with each movement until you reach the far wall, then leap backwards. Takes about seventy reps to cross the room twice."

Forward-backward jumping jacks gave Forbes's abdominal wall and lower back a more vigorous workout than he expected. He became winded quickly crossing the room once. He had to stop to catch his breath before doing them backwards, which was easier.

"Now we skip rope. Increases your wind and builds your timing," Hitchcock said as he demonstrated, smoothly skipping over each turn of the rope as it whisked the floor, using a variety of skipping patterns.

In seconds Forbes again became winded. His feet kept stepping on the rope and one foot or the other got entangled. Panting heavily, he sought a place to sit down, but Hitchcock drove him on.

"No stopping. Pushups next. Let's do thirty-five to get blood flowing in our arms and shoulders. We'll do 'em together." Forbes hesitated. He had been taught that high repetitions reduce muscle mass rather than increase it, and size is what impresses people. But he obeyed Hitchcock, who counted out pushups, slow and full length. Forbes collapsed after twenty-five reps, arms shaking.

"Time to wrap our hands. We do this to protect our hands before the gloves go on. Hold your right hand out, palm down, fingers spread," Hitchcock directed.

Forbes used the time Hitchcock spent wrapping his hands to catch his breath. Hitchcock wrapped a two-inch wide strip of cloth many times across the knuckles, between the fingers and around the wrists for support.

Having his hands wrapped for the first time was a new experience for Forbes. He felt the tingle and the rush of excitement real fighters must feel. Hitchcock put the club's red leather sixteen-ounce gloves with the

Everlast brand name on the wrists over the wrappings on Forbes's hands.

Banging his gloves together to get used to the feel of them, Forbes said, "These feel like pillows, Roger. How could anybody get hurt with these?"

"Hard-hitters like Rocky Marciano, Joe Louis, and Boone Kirkman have broken their opponents' jaws and ribs while wearing these," Hitchcock replied.

"Who? Yeah? Well, I can hardly believe it," Forbes said, banging his gloved hands together. He felt what real fighters must feel, a primeval thrill, an eagerness to get it on, to sweat, conquer and shed blood in hand-to-hand battle. For the first time in his life, Forbes felt real, and his admiration of Hitchcock soared.

"Now that your hands are protected, to the heavy bag."

Hitchcock explained proper stance, foot and hand position, leading with his left, the use of the left jab, the right cross, the left hook, right hook, and the uppercut. It embarrassed Forbes that in spite of his upper body size from using weight machines, he moved clumsily, became winded easily, and his punches lacked power.

Next, Hitchcock strapped a padded helmet with faceguard on Forbes' head to protect him from what was coming.

Forbes tried to hide his surprise at the size, shape and definition of Hitchcock's upper arms and shoulders when he removed his sweatshirt. Hitchcock taped his own hands, put on a pair of gloves, but no helmet, which he took to mean Hitchcock didn't take him seriously.

"Let's get in the ring and go over what we covered today."

Forbes stepped through the ropes wishing he had boxed during his youth.

Hitchcock extended his hands in front of his body, palms out, "when I call out which hand to punch with, hit the glove I extend to you. Left jab!"

Forbes punched with his left, but with weak impact.

"Again!" Hitchcock commanded, holding up his gloved right hand to be hit. "Now left-right to my left hand!" Forbes did, but his clenched fists robbed him of power and speed. Angry and embarrassed, Forbes tried harder, throwing punches out of order.

"Okay, stop," Hitchcock ordered, but Forbes didn't stop. Thinking he would impress Hitchcock with his strength, he swung at Hitchcock's head as soon as Hitchcock put his hands down. Hitchcock slipped aside. Forbes's punch missed, and the momentum caused him to fall.

"For all your superfluous muscle, you hit like a girl, Mark, because you train the wrong way."

Forbes blushed with embarrassment.

"Let's do some defense now," Hitchcock said. "Hands up! I showed you how to guard yourself."

Forbes shielded his face with his gloves, Hitchcock's first punch, a left jab, came in so fast that though he saw it coming, he couldn't react in time. It landed on Forbes's gloves so hard it knocked his gloves into his face, almost knocking him down. Forbes staggered backward. Only the ropes kept him from falling.

Hitchcock closed in and slipped a right uppercut between Forbes's gloves, clipping him on the chin. Forbes's lights dimmed for a moment as he fell back against the ropes again.

Forbes regained his footing and threw an overhand right at Hitchcock with all his might. Hitchcock slipped under it unscathed, causing Forbes to lose balance and almost fall as he staggered past Hitchcock. Mustering his strength, Forbes struggled to his feet and charged Hitchcock like an embarrassed, enraged child, throwing wild windmill punches.

Stepping aside, Hitchcock nailed Forbes with a right hook to the side of his head as he sailed by and collapsed again.

"Get up!" Hitchcock demanded; the friendliness gone from his voice.

Panting heavily, Forbes got up, one knee at a time. He wobbled like a drunk as he faced Hitchcock, whom he hadn't been able to touch even once.

He stepped forward, circling to his right, to avoid the power of Hitchcock's right but Hitchcock dropped him again with a left jab to the forehead of his helmet.

Forbes muttered curses at Hitchcock as he struggled to his feet. Another left jab from Hitchcock sent him sprawling into the ropes. He could hardly believe how Hitchcock's fist arrived in his face before he could react. He advanced, muttering threats.

"What did you say, *officer*?" Hitchcock demanded, saying the last word with spitting contempt.

Heaving and gasping, Forbes stammered, "I said – I said – I'm going to kill you, you – "

Hitchcock landed a hard right upon his upper left shoulder where the arm enters the shoulder socket, striking a key nerve. Forbes's left hand dropped to his side, useless, as he cried out in pain.

"Okay, okay, you win! Stop! I'm done, you bast – " Hitchcock struck his shoulder again. "Let me go," Forbes begged.

"First, apologize. See how easily you are beaten?" Hitchcock demanded. "Do it now!"

"I – I'm sorry," he gasped, holding his right hand over his left shoulder. "I'm in the wrong, Roger. I'm sorry. Please – forgive me and help me."

"Prove it first. Tell me about your dealings with Bostwick. I want the truth!"

Forbes, gasping for air, answered between breaths. "He – Bostwick – promised – job... Warrant Detail – so I could be – with family nights and weekends – if I report – on you guys to him."

"So, what did you do?"

Forbes caught his breath before he replied. "I told him about the Super Vel ammo after I saw Wooten and Allard loading it into their guns."

"You traitor!" Hitchcock shouted. "Those guys are fellow officers. Our brothers. They have families, wives and kids at home who depend on them! You *knew*

144

Bostwick would fire them for the slightest reason. What else did you tell Bostwick?" Hitchcock demanded, seething now.

"He asked me about the fight at the Village Inn. After I told him, he told me to lie, to say you used excessive force on Beecham, but I refused. I would be dead or a vegetable if not for you."

Hitchcock removed their gloves. He went to the sheet of paper on the clipboard and pen he brought.

"Here's the deal—I'm writing what you told me into a statement and you're signing it. I keep the statement and you keep your job with the Warrant Detail, but you start looking for another line of work."

Forbes, still panting and holding his left shoulder with his right hand, nodded agreement.

"You have ninety days to resign. If you're still here after that, I give the statement to Captain Delstra. Deal?"

Forbes hesitated before he said, "Deal, Roger. I'm sorry...and ashamed."

"This is the way to move forward and make a new start with a minimum of damage."

Hitchcock wrote the statement. Forbes read it out loud, initial each paragraph and signed it at the bottom.

"Why did you do such a thing, Mark?"

"Personal reasons. I can't, and won't, say."

"One more thing. I don't want to see or hear of you abusing or manhandling a prisoner again, in any way. If I do, this statement goes to Captain Delstra. Got it?"

"I agree," Forbes said, holding his limp left arm with

his right hand. "What about my shoulder?"

"You'll recover in about an hour. We better leave before the kids and their coaches arrive."

After Forbes dressed, Hitchcock told him, "I don't approve of how you do your job, but I respect you for humbling yourself today. You asked for help, so I will say your resistance training program is wrong. Your arms are bigger than mine, yet your punches are weak, and you tire easily. You're strong, but you're not fit."

"I'm not?" Forbes asked, surprised.

"Check out how most boxers are built. Even heavyweight champs like Muhammad Ali, George Foreman, Joe Louis or Rocky Marciano were lean, not muscle-bound pretty-boys. And, you weren't in the military, but real fighters like the Green Berets and Army Rangers aren't muscle-bound freaks either."

"How should I train, then?"

"Use your bodyweight more than weights to build strength and endurance at the same time. Do multiple sets of high repetition sit-ups, pushups and pull-ups. Your arms will slim a bit, but you'll be surprised at how much more functional strength and speed will result. Strengthen your heart with jumping jacks, wind sprints and skipping rope. Work out on a heavy bag for about twenty minutes at least once a week."

"How often should I work out?"

"In Golden Gloves, we trained five days a week for at least an hour after school and we competed in three-round matches on Saturdays. To qualify for the

Olympics, they accelerated the pace. We could keep that pace up because we worked up to it and we were young. Recovery time takes longer as we age. Do as I described for about a half hour every other day, and start slow."

"Thanks, Roger," Forbes said. "You opened my eyes to many things today and I see why you conquered Beecham so quickly."

Hitchcock read the statement after Forbes left:

> *To Whom it may concern:*
>
> *I, Mark Forbes, a police officer with the Bellevue Police Department, state the following of my own free will:*
> *Last September, I was being beaten by Crawford Beecham while trying to arrest him for assaulting off-duty Sergeant Baxter and his wife. Officer Hitchcock saved my life.*
> *Lt. Bostwick offered me a position in the Warrant Detail if I falsely alleged that Hitchcock used excessive force against Beecham. I refused. In December, Lt. Bostwick offered me the same job if I would inform on my fellow officers.*
> *For personal reasons I accepted. Later I told him about the officers who were using other than department-issue ammunition.*
> *I deeply regret my actions.*
>
> *Signed: Mark J. Forbes.*
> *January 1971*

CHAPTER TWENTY-TWO
The Friday Routine

SCHEDULE PERMITTING, HITCHCOCK always had lunch with his mother on Fridays. He arrived at her home in Medina minutes after he left the Boys Club, expecting to take her to the elegant Rhododendron Room at Frederick & Nelson store in Bellevue Square.

"We'll eat here today, instead of going out, to save you time," Myrna said as she hugged him.

"Sure, Mom. I'm hungry," he said, liking the idea of a home-cooked meal.

She reached across the table and patted his wrist as he took his first bite of baked salmon. "I enjoyed meeting your Allie at Christmas, son. Such natural poise and class. She's beautiful inside and out, and her little boy is precious."

He smiled at the mention of Allie's name. "I'm glad you liked her, Mom," he said between bites.

"My question is, are you prepared to take on a ready-made family?"

Hitchcock stopped his fork mid-air. "Who said I'm going to marry her, Mom?"

Myrna smiled her knowing-mother-smile. "The way you are with her and she with you, the way her son is with you and the way she greeted me, it's obvious."

"Does this mean you're off the Emily Chatterton thing?"

"I had only your best interests in mind," she said, a bit defensive. "I want you to enjoy the same stable family life your father and I had. I thought Emily would give you that until I met Allie. That's when I realized I was wrong about Emily."

He put his fork down in surprise. He couldn't remember his mother admitting to being wrong about anything.

"I could tell something else about Allie," she said. "She won't sleep with you because you're not married, right?"

"How did you know? Surely you didn't ask or say anything to her! Or did you—Mom?" he blurted, worry in his voice.

"Of course not! I'm your mother. I would never embarrass you. Your dad and I were virgins when we married."

"I never knew that about you and Dad, but I assumed it was true."

"Waiting made our marriage strong, Roger. It gave us a deeper respect for each other. Your dad was as handsome a man as you are. Many girls wanted him, but he wanted only me. We shared a sense of destiny. By waiting, we established a foundation of trust and respect for our marriage that withstood the storms of life until Ted's passing."

In his inner man he knew his mother was right. His parents' marriage had been unbreakable. Each of his many romantic entanglements seemed right at first, but every one ended in futility.

"I haven't proposed to her, Mom."

"She'll accept when you do, but don't dally. Someone else might snatch her up. There's no way other eligible men aren't interested in her. Little kid or not, Allie's a catch like no other."

Hitchcock nodded in silent agreement, noting that his mother sounded like Bill Chace. *Mom hasn't been talking to Bill, or has she?*

"So, what else is new with my son?"

"I volunteered to teach boxing to junior high age boys at the Bellevue Boys Club once a week."

"Good on you," she said. "The boys of this younger generation need men like you. Their dads aren't home as they should be, and they aren't in charge when they are. The discipline they'll learn will strengthen them. Is that where you were this afternoon, giving lessons?"

"I gave a private lesson to an adult."

"Oh – an adult. Did he learn much?"

"Yes, as a matter of fact, he learned a lot, rather quickly. I'm surprised at how much he learned. A second lesson he won't need – I hope."

CHAPTER TWENTY-THREE
The Foreign Visitor

THE FOLLOWING FRIDAY, a dapper Japanese man deplaned at the Seattle-Tacoma International Airport. He was in his forties, dressed in an immaculate brown pinstripe suit and shined shoes to match. No one met him as he entered the airport. His stiff, professional manner and tailor-made suit induced the car rental agent to rent him a Lincoln Continental at no additional cost.

The visitor smirked as he passed the sign on the I-5 freeway that read: WILL THE LAST PERSON TO LEAVE SEATTLE PLEASE TURN OUT THE LIGHTS?

He followed the freeway signs to Bellevue. Using a map, he found the two-story glass building of Pacific Aero Engineering on a hilltop, overlooking the I-405-Highway 10 interchange.

The visitor positioned himself a discreet distance from the cyclone-fenced parking lot. Using a 500mm telephoto lens, he photographed the premises, the license numbers of employees' vehicles, and the employees leaving and returning from their lunch break.

He passed a black-and-white police car as he left, and waved for the officer to stop.

"Pardon me, officer," he said in measured, too-perfect English, and a slight bow. "Could you please direct me to the Planning Department of Bellevue City Hall?"

HE DISCREETLY PHOTOGRAPHED the blueprints of the Pacific Aero Engineering building with a tiny Minox spy camera. He then returned to Pacific Aero Engineering in time to see the employees leaving for the night and how the building was secured.

Dressed casually in slacks, cashmere sweater and sport coat, he resumed surveillance early the next morning. He remained past sunset, verifying with timestamped photographs that, except for the janitorial service arrival at 2:00 p.m. and departure at 4:00 p.m., Pacific Aero Engineering's building was closed and unguarded on Saturdays.

As unobtrusively as he came, the Japanese national left on an evening flight for Tokyo.

† † †

A WEEK PASSED. For a Saturday the morning had been quiet. Ray Packard, the District Five car, responded to a Dead On Arrival call at 10:00 a.m.

Minutes later, Hitchcock received a call in Packard's district: *"Silent alarm at Pacific Aero Engineering at 11820 SE 32nd–Code Two."*

He arrived in seconds. The chain-link fence gate was locked, the parking lot inside the fenced area was empty and the interior building lights were out. A tan, unoccupied, late model Oldsmobile sedan was parked on the street, facing the fence. The warmth of its hood indicated arrival minutes ago.

He called in the plate number, scaled the six-foot fence and dropped into the enclosed parking lot. The lights in the lobby were out. From around the corner, he peeked into the dimly lit lobby. A tiny red light mounted flush with the ceiling blinked rapidly, indicating an intruder. Whoever entered the building had a key, for he saw no sign of forced entry. He drew his gun and slipped out of sight around the corner when he heard a door slam inside.

Seconds later a middle-aged, slightly overweight man with a receding hairline, wearing khaki pants and a red plaid Pendleton wool shirt, carrying a brown leather briefcase, exited the front door, locking it with a key.

"Police–stop right there," Hitchcock ordered. The man seemed appropriately alarmed.

"Oh, thank God it's you, officer," the man said, seeming relieved to see a police uniform. He put his hand on his chest as if to calm his heart and catch his breath.

"I'm glad you're on the job. I work here, I came by to pick up some things from my office to work on for a Monday deadline. Here's my key to the building, and my company ID card."

Though the man and his ID card seemed credible, something wasn't right. "Well, Mr. Clymer. You seem pretty legit except for two small details. If you have a key to the building, you should also have a key to the gate," he said, intentionally not mentioning the alarm. "And, where's your car, Mr. Clymer?"

He pointed at the Oldsmobile.

"And your key to the gate is...?"

"I forgot it," Clymer replied, fidgeting, "I live in Renton, a long drive from here, so I climbed the fence. May I go now?"

Walker arrived. Hitchcock held up his hand as a signal to wait.

"Not just yet. Hand your briefcase to the other officer so you don't drop it, then we'll climb over the fence."

Clymer was overweight. He ascended the cyclone fence to the top with difficulty, handed the briefcase to Walker, then eased himself to the ground. Hitchcock followed. He told Clymer to wait in front of Walker's patrol car as he switched to F2 and keyed his mic.

"Call the home phone on file for the owner of Pacific Aero Engineering. Ask if a Richard Clymer works for the company."

Clymer's fidgeting increased by the minute. Finally

Records called back: *The company president, Tim Rollins, is on the phone. He says Richard Clymer did work for the company but was fired over six months ago. He says Clymer has no business being in the building.*

Hitchcock confronted Clymer with what his former boss said.

Clymer said nothing.

"You are under arrest for investigation of second-degree burglary, Mr. Clymer."

The color drained out of his face as he listened to and acknowledged his Constitutional rights, his voice a notch above a whisper.

† † †

HITCHCOCK SHOVED A paper in front of Clymer after booking. "You can make this easy or difficult, Mr. Clymer. Sign this voluntary search warrant so I can see what's in your briefcase, or you can cool your jets here for several hours while I round up a judge off a golf course to give me a search warrant."

Clymer signed but refused to talk. Hitchcock put him in a holding cell.

Tim Rollins, the company president, arrived.

"These are highly classified documents," Rollins said when he saw the contents in Clymer's briefcase. "We subcontract to Boeing on military projects. Richard Clymer was one of our top engineers. His work deteriorated so sharply last year I had no choice but to let him go. The company gave him a very fair severance package."

"What caused the change?" Hitchcock asked.

"His wife left him after years of uncontrollable gambling devastated their finances. He hid this from us for years."

"How serious is this, Mr. Rollins?"

"This is espionage by a foreign government to obtain military aircraft plans. Boeing contracts with the federal government and subs some of the work to us. Without disclosing more details, it will suffice to say Richard Clymer has sold out our country to a foreign power."

For a moment, Hitchcock was too stunned to speak. "Exactly how did his job performance decline?" he asked.

"I never noticed any signs of drug or alcohol problems," Rollins replied, "but he disappeared a lot during work hours, he missed more and more meetings and deadlines. Eventually I hired a private investigator to tail him. That's how I found out about his addiction to the racetrack at Longacres on company time, which is where his money went—betting on the horses."

Hitchcock looked at Rollins. "Which begs the question, how did Clymer get involved with agents of a foreign power?"

"Good question," Rollins said. "They had to be spying on us for our military technology. For sure the FBI will jump on this. What did Richard say to you?"

"Refused."

"Besides harming our country, he put our company in extreme jeopardy. I'd like to talk to him. I was an officer in Army intelligence in Vietnam."

Hitchcock led Rollins to the interview room. He stood outside the door, listening.

"I'm shocked and disappointed, Richard. What brought you to this?" Hitchcock heard Rollins ask.

"Money. Linda left me."

"And the kids?"

"She took them too."

"You're a fine engineer, Richard. Letting you go wasn't easy for me. Is the money you got worth this?"

After a pause, Clymer whispered, "No."

"Is it possible you've been inside the office other times after I fired you?"

Long pause. "It's possible."

"Are you doing this for a country, or a company?"

"The first."

"Which country, Richard? Tell me."

"I'm dead if I do."

"Give me the first letter of the name of that country, Richard, and we're done."

"J."

"Were you involved with these people before I fired you, Richard?"

After a long pause, Clymer replied, "Yes."

"I KNOW YOU will have to notify the FBI of this as part of your duty. As company president I will do the same,"

Rollins told Hitchcock. "I will personally report this to the FBI and Boeing Security today. It will probably mean the end of our company, but that is out of my hands. And yes, as company president I want to press charges."

HITCHCOCK SHOOK HIS head in dismay after he booked Clymer into the King County Jail. He had become the first officer in Bellevue's history to make a field arrest for industrial espionage. As distinctive as the arrest was, the scope of the evil facing him, his family, his country bewildered him.

He likened himself to a ship on a stormy sea.

CHAPTER TWENTY-FOUR
A Time to Die?

Eastgate
Sunday - 4:00 A.M.

DRY, COOL WEATHER and radio silence made for a perfect morning to hunt for what the night shift might have missed—a stolen car, a commercial burglary, a dead body. Like a Bloodhound padding along a forest trail, its nose to the ground, Hitchcock probed Eastgate's nooks and crannies with his window down and the heater off to hear better.

Finding nothing, he and Walker placed their orders and sat down with fresh coffee when Art's opened. They stared at each other and shook their heads when the phone rang.

"Nobody calls Art's this early except the station," Walker predicted.

"Station's calling you guys!" Art yelled.

Hitchcock took the call. "Alarm at Safeway," he

grumbled.

"Second time this week. At least it's Sunday," Walker muttered.

"Meaning what?"

"Almost nobody goes to church anymore, so there's no traffic," Walker said.

"Yeah, well, let's go in one car. You drive."

"Hangover?"

He shook his head. "I was out late with Allie."

"Yep–you're hung over. I'll drive."

† † †

THEY ENTERED THE alley behind the from the north end, headlights off. Hitchcock felt a tinge of alarm when he saw the taillights of a full-size American sedan heading away, around the south end of the store.

"Who do you think that is?"

"Somebody dropping off an employee. The roll-up door is open and there's a bakery truck at the dock, Walker said. "This is the regular time for deliveries and employees."

"Guess so." He paused, reflecting on the uneasiness he still felt, then shook his head. "I'll let Dispatch know we're here. Let's check it quick. I want to get back to our coffee."

"I'm with you on that."

They climbed the short ladder to the loading dock and sauntered through the large rollup door into the dimly lighted refrigerated storage area of the store, where cases of produce and canned food were stacked on both sides, thumbs hooked into their gun belts, looking for the employees.

The further in they ventured, the more uneasy Hitchcock became. Something was very wrong. His stomach churned as he and Walker stopped, listening for but not hearing the usual sounds of employees talking or moving cases of produce. Somewhere on the main floor a phone was ringing nonstop.

Hitchcock split off from Walker to check the offices upstairs. An adrenalin boost hit him when he saw the door of the first office at the top of the stairs standing open, ransacked, the phone yanked out of the wall, wire dangling. Goosebumps covered his flesh. He drew his gun. "Ira!"

"Yo!"

"We got a good alarm here! Office ransacked, employees missing. Suspects may still be inside! Watch yourself!"

"Got it!" Walker yelled back, his voice raspy and hoarse. Gun in hand, he pressed his back to the wall.

The phone kept ringing.

At the top of the stairs, Hitchcock listened for voices. He heard none, which meant the offices were empty as they should be this early.

Still sensing danger, he moved down the hall, sweeping each office holding his gun in a two-hand grip, expecting an ambush at any time. He heard faint sounds of movement as he neared the fourth office. It was empty. The sounds continued. He followed them to a storage closet at the end of the hall. He threw the door open, holding his revolver at low-ready.

Three terrified men were huddled inside. Two he recognized as employees. The third man wore the uniform of the bakery company truck parked outside.

"Anyone hurt?" he asked.

The three exchanged glances. "Just lucky to be alive, officer," one of them said, his voice shaking.

"What happened?"

The bakery truck driver spoke up. "Two guys with guns were here when I arrived. They ordered me into the store at gun point. They took us upstairs, ripped the phone out of the wall and took the manager, Mr. Dawson, downstairs with them."

"That's right, officer," a store employee said, his eyes bulging. "The first one took me to the upstairs office, forced me to open the safe, which he cleaned out. Then he took us back here and locked us in."

"Then what happened?" Hitchcock asked.

"They told us to keep quiet or they would shoot us. I became even more frightened when they took Mr. Dawson. I thought they'd kill him for sure, then us."

† † †

DOWNSTAIRS, WALKER FOUND the manager's safe open, the office ransacked, the manager bound and gagged, sitting on the floor, back against the wall.

"Are you harmed, Mr. Dawson?" Walker asked as

he removed the cloth gag from his mouth and untied him.

Scott Dawson, a man in his early thirties, gasped for air, holding his right hand over his heart, as if that would slow it.

"They were about to kill me after they said they wouldn't if I opened the safe for them." He said between breaths, his chest heaving.

Walker sat on his haunches in front of him. "Take a deep breath and let it out slowly, Mr. Dawson, then another. As soon as you catch your breath, tell me what happened."

Hitchcock entered. "I was a medic in the Army," he said as he pressed his finger on Dawson's neck to check his pulse, then his pupils with a flashlight. "Your pulse is fast, Mr. Dawson. Given what happened here today, it should be. You'll be okay, but the ER docs will probably give you a sedative. Can you answer a couple questions for us?"

Dawson nodded.

"What, or who set off the alarm?"

Breathing openmouthed, Dawson replied, "I-I was in the-the upstairs office when they came in. One-one of my guys must have t-triggered it."

"Then what happened?"

"They s-stuck a gun-a gun in my ribs and took me to the safe downstairs. Th-they said they w-would shoot me unless I opened it, so I did. One tied me up—"

Dawson broke down crying, rubbing his eyes with

trembling hands.

"Wh–while one s-scooped all the money from the safe into a b–bag," he gasped, "th–then the other aimed his gun at m-my face when the phone started ringing. I–I begged him not to shoot me–I have a family. He asked me who was calling. I t-told them the p–police station always sends two officers before they call the store. That's w-when they put a gag in my mouth and left."

Hitchcock and Walker exchanged glances. "The car we saw leaving as we arrived was them," Hitchcock said.

Having secured the scene with barrier tape and turned early customers away, they took statements from the victims until a team of detectives relieved them.

† † †

THEY RETURNED TO Art's. Hitchcock ordered ham, four eggs basted, toast buttered, hash browns crisp. Walker drank coffee in the stunned silence of the lucky-to-be-alive. He watched Hitchcock cut into the slice of ham.

"If we'd arrived seconds earlier, we'd be dead. How can you eat after we were almost killed..." Walker's voice trailed off. His face was unreadable.

Hitchcock nodded as he ate. "We dodged the scythe of the Grim Reaper by a whisker that time for sure," he said off-handedly. "Not the first time, won't be the last–not for cops in these times."

CHAPTER TWENTY-FIVE
The Safeway Effect

HITCHCOCK'S EASY COOLNESS after a close brush with death stunned Walker. "The way we walked in, so sure it was another false alarm, after all the warnings and news stories Jack read to us at shift briefings, the boredom of routine patrol *still* almost got us killed, Roger."

"Lesson learned," Hitchcock said, wolfing down his hash browns.

"Lesson?"

"As lax as we were, we weren't killed and neither were the employees. It's because our numbers weren't up yet."

"I'm surprised you're so flippant."

"Think of it as a wake-up call, a lucky break."

The five-hundred-yard stare in Walker's eyes was as if he didn't hear Hitchcock's comment. At last he said, "Your sixth sense or whatever you call it, kicked in, but I ignored it. I took too much for granted—I almost got us killed."

Hitchcock stopped eating and gave his partner a level stare. "Don't go beating yourself up over it. The blame is mine. I didn't heed it either."

† † †

HITCHCOCK WASN'T SHAKEN. He'd been through close calls with death too many times. But it got him thinking. But he knew his luck with the law of averages would someday run out. Until now he'd been living day-to-day, month-to-month with no plan, no thought of the future, as if his supply of tomorrows would never end. *There's a last day for every living thing. How will I stack up in the final accounting?*

He made no stops and received no calls for the rest of the shift. His hands were cold as he unlocked his El Camino and started the engine. He smiled to see Jamie waiting for him in the driveway, wagging his tail when he arrived at his digs. His cabana felt like someone else's abode.

He walked around the outside of Doc and Ethel's house and his cabana, Jamie at his side, checking for signs of entry, finding none. He changed clothes and left. Taking Jamie along, he headed for the Pancake Corral.

† † †

BILL CHACE WAS ringing out the last customer when Hitchcock walked in, his eyes searching for Allie. "Hiya, Hitch, your sweetheart's getting off in a minute. Grab a seat while I get you a cup."

"Thanks, Bill," he replied mechanically as his eyes found Allie wiping down tables in the back. The mere sight of her had an uplifting effect on him. She smiled when she saw him but kept working until she reached his table. "Excuse me, sir, I must wipe your table off so I can go home," she said softly as she bent over him, her face radiating love.

Her presence made him forget his close call with death. She came within inches of him, bent over, wiping the table with a damp cloth. He planted a quick kiss on her cheek.

She straightened up and touched her cheek. "Oh, sir! I am but a waitress here and still on duty," she said, a broad smile turning up her lovely lips, hot love burning in her eyes as she whispered, "Silly boy!" Hitchcock glanced over her shoulder at pairs of smiling eyes peeking at them from the back.

HE FOLLOWED ALLIE home. He visited with her mother and played with Trevor. When her mother went home, and Trevor took a nap, he and Allie smooched on the couch.

In the early evening, the aromas of food on the stove, the sight of Allie working in the kitchen, he began to assess himself. After the meal they returned to the couch.

"I'm in love with you, Roger," she told him in a matter-of-fact way.

"Let's spend the day together this Tuesday."

"Okay," she said, hiding her disappointment that he didn't respond to her declaration of love. "Tell me what we're doing. Shall I bring Trevor?

"Ask your mom to watch Trevor all day."

"What time will you be here?"

"Nine. Wear a swimsuit under warm clothes, hiking boots or running shoes, and bring a couple towels."

"What? Where are we—"

"Be ready at nine, sharp."

† † †

Monday - 4:15 A.M.

A LIGHT RAIN began when Hitchcock and Walker met car-to-car at the back of The Steak Out. The remoteness in Walker's eyes prompted Hitchcock to ask, "How are you doing with what happened yesterday, Ira?"

Walker stared out his windshield, hands on the steering wheel. "Our uniform shirts should have 'Shoot Me First' printed on them, front and back."

"What do you mean?"

"The criminals have the advantage. We wear uniforms and drive marked cars, which makes citizens feel safe. But they make us easy targets for anybody who wants to shoot one of us just to see his name in the news."

"These are bad times for cops," Hitchcock agreed.

Walker's face revealed the stress he was under. He looked at Hitchcock. "My turn—how are you doing with what happened yesterday?"

Hitchcock shrugged. "It wasn't our day to die."

"That's still your take on it?" Walker asked.

"In a firefight in 'Nam, a soldier on either side of me got killed, but not me. The three of us had drank whiskey together the night before. It was their day to die, not mine. That's it."

"Maybe the difference between us is your combat experience. You've killed and seen killing, like Otis, Sherman and some others."

"It changed me."

"Did you ever wonder what's on the other side of this life?"

"Dead is dead, Ira."

"Well, what almost happened made *me* think about it a lot," Walker sighed. "I'm single now, but I got my kids. What would happen to them if those guys killed me yesterday? Who would make sure my kids receive my pension or anything else I leave them?"

"Certainly not your ex."

"My point exactly. By not having my affairs in order, I've been living in a fool's paradise, as if I'm invincible and there'll never be a last day."

"What are you going to do?"

"Buy life insurance on myself for my kids. My brother'll have power of attorney so my ex can't get any of it. I'm also having a simple will drawn up by an attorney."

"Insurance premiums will shrink your take-home

pay."

"It'll be worth the peace of mind."

"You remember how my name is spelled?"

Walker looked at him, puzzled. "Huh?"

"So I can be your beneficiary, too."

Walker finally chuckled.

"After you've got your ducks lined up, then what?"

"Between calls we wear our detective hats. We find Mike Smith before he kills any more people. We nail the drug-dealing broad who works at Albertsons, and we solve the case of who killed Stacey Brock, even if her mom won't help us because she's in on it. With only five detectives for a town this big, they'll never have enough time to get to the bottom of it."

"That's a tall order, but I'm in."

AT METKE FORD downtown, he traded his El Camino in on a charcoal gray '69 Jeep Wagoneer, four-wheel-drive, loaded. The previous owner had gone all in to customize it. Oversized off-road tires, heavy duty diamond plate bumpers, a power-take-off winch with a hundred feet of steel cable mounted behind the front bumper, towing package, lift kit, CB radio and roof rack.

This'll get me wherever I want to go, he thought. *Now for Allie.*

CHAPTER TWENTY-SIX
The Secret Cavern

COLD, BLUSTERY WINDS buffeted him and Allie as they went downstairs from her apartment the next morning. She expressed surprise and approval as she looked the Wagoneer over. In the back seat, Jamie woofed and wagged his tail at the sight of her.

"Ah—I'm glad to see you too, my good friend," Allie said as she rubbed the top and sides of his head.

"I traded my El Camino in for it," he explained before she could ask. "The former owner got laid off. I just took over the payments."

"This is a real rig. Where're we going, may I ask?"

"You brought your swimsuit?"

"I'm wearing it like you said," she replied.

"So am I."

"Today is my birthday," she said cheerfully.

"You're twenty-one now."

"How did you know, or should I ask?"

"I check out all my women," he said playfully. "Us

cops gotta be careful, you know."

Allie gave him a lively slap on his upper arm. "I'll bet you do," she said. "We have muffins and coffee for us but what about Jamie?"

"I brought treats for him too."

They left Highway 10 at the town of North Bend and headed north on a two-lane asphalt road through thick stands of evergreens and leafless elm and alder trees until the pavement ended.

The rough road narrowed to a dirt-and-rock path which ascended sharply into a dense mountain forest of Douglas Fir and cedar trees. At a sharp turn he stopped and got out to turn the front locking hubs to engage the four-wheel-drive unit.

"Buckle your seat belt," he said.

In low gear the Wagoneer crawled, clawed and bounced its way up a steep incline over deep ruts and rocks under a canopy of evergreen trees so thick they dimmed the mid-morning sunlight.

Allie held on, belted into her seat, gripping a loop of nylon strap fastened to the ceiling and bracing her hand against the dash with her left hand.

"Where are we going, and why did you say to wear my swimsuit? It's winter," she asked, her voice halting between words as the Jeep bucked and twisted its way up the trail.

"You'll see," he said.

Higher and higher the Jeep clambered, with saplings scraping both sides until they came to a level grassy meadow with a towering dark gray rock cliff on the other side.

"We're here," he said.

He opened the door for Allie, grabbed his military surplus backpack out of the back and let Jamie out.

Taking her by the hand, he led her to an opening in the rock cliff.

The warmth of steam met them as he led her through the opening into a natural hot spring spa surrounded by a rock ledge. Shafts of daylight shone through the openings in the rock ceiling. Allie let go of his hand as she gasped.

"Roger! Is this for real? I feel like I'm in a movie! How did you know about this place?"

"I found it years ago on my explorations in these mountains. Come on, the water will be perfect."

He shucked his boots and clothes to his swim trunks and slipped into the warm water before he started shivering in the cold. Allie stood, openmouthed in surprise at their surroundings and at his lean, sinewy physique.

"What are you waiting for—a written invitation?" he teased.

Allie stripped down to the purple bikini under her jeans and sweater. She passed through the steam and eased into the deliciously warm waters. The glimpse he got of her before she entered the water was enough to satisfy his curiosity—her hourglass figure was exquisite. *She's got everything in the right place,* he observed with pleasure. The water was a little over four feet deep. He took her in his arms. She wrapped her arms around his neck as they talked delightedly, up to their necks in the hot water while Jamie stood guard, his off-duty .38 within arm's reach.

He led her to the shallow water.

"Stand here." He withdrew something from the pocket of his trunks and hid it in his hand. He saw Allie's eyes bulge as he knelt in front of her.

"The next time we come here, I want it to be on our honeymoon," he said, looking up at her. Tears formed in her eyes. "I am totally in love with you, Allie. I have been all along. I cannot live without you any longer. Will you please marry me?" he asked, looking up at her as he held forth a diamond-encrusted engagement ring set in white gold.

"What did you say?" she asked through a burst of sobbing.

He laughed. "Will you please marry me, Allie?"

"Yes, yes, oh yes, Roger. I will, I do. I will be your wife forever," she gushed.

He put the engagement ring on her right ring finger, they embraced, kissed, then slipped back into the warm waters of the secret hot springs, excited, talking of plans and desires.

"We'll have kids, and I want boys..." Allie told him. "But you can't have me until we're married. We've waited this long. I want it to be the right way, so it will last."

"I will wait," he told her. "But I don't want much delay."

"Nor do I."

"So, what do you think, a couple months?"

"No, my love. Three *weeks*, no more," she said, surprising him.

"People will think this is a shotgun wedding, being so quick," he said.

"So what? They will anyway when you knock me up on our honeymoon," she laughed.

"Happy Birthday, too, by the way," he added, at which she launched into his arms.

† † †

SEAGULLS CIRCLED OVER them, squawking and cawing, wanting their baskets of fish and chips as they sat outside at Ivar's Fish Bar on the Seattle waterfront the next day.

"We're rushing it through so fast they'll think I'm pregnant, honey," Allie said, flirtation in the voice.

"We can skip the wait for our marriage license applications and elope to Idaho, baby," he said, as she wrote a guest list on a napkin.

"Nope."

"You're forgetting something," he said.

"I am? What?"

"Knowing the date and place would help me be there on time," he said.

Allie leaned back and laughed. "Of course! We

didn't even talk about that. How could I forget such minor details as the date and place!"

"Aren't we a pair of eager-beavers," he said good humoredly.

"I want a *church wedding*, conducted by a pastor, a man of God, not a cold courthouse *ceremony* with a judge, like Glendon insisted on. I want to be married in the right way, in the church I grew up in."

"Your wish is my command."

"I'm holding you to it," she said, using her reply from last Christmas. "Let's go to Renton."

"Renton?"

"My hometown. I want you to see the church we'll use. I'll direct you. It's on our way, sorta."

"Renton here we come," he said happily.

"I want five boys," she said.

CHAPTER TWENTY-SEVEN
Taking Charge

Thursday - 3:45 A.M.
Shift Briefing

SERGEANT BREEN STOOD at the podium, quieter than usual. "Before I read Patrol updates, here's news affecting everyone," he said. "The second wave of Boeing layoffs are underway. These will be the deepest cuts yet. Public anger is just beginning. It's on the news that a couple Boeing engineers who got laid off put up a billboard sign beside the I-5 freeway which says, 'Will the last person to leave Seattle please turn out the lights?'.

"I saw it," Otis said. "How could they pay for a sign like that if they just got laid off?"

Breen glanced at Otis, then around the squad room. "Makes you wonder, huh? A lot of homes and cars will be going back to the banks. Savings will be used up. The rise we've seen in family beefs, false reports for insurance money, and suicides will increase. Let's be open for ways to help those who are suffering when we're out there."

"What can we do to help?" an officer asked.

"The Chief's office is putting together a list of churches that are offering to help people in need keep food on the table. I'll make copies available for each of you as soon as it's out."

† † †

THE LATEST PATROL updates amounted to an armed robbery, six residential burglaries, two commercial burglaries, another runaway juvenile, and another drug overdose death in the last two days.

The squad's mood was solemn. Without a word they collected their gear and headed to their patrol cars. Everyone had a relative or friend who is or would be caught in the spreading economic tailspin.

Having patrolled Eastgate until daylight, probing parked cars at closed bars, parks, motels and schools, finding nothing, Hitchcock met Walker at Art's.

"How did your days off go?" Walker asked as he poured himself a mug of coffee.

"Eventful," Hitchcock said as he poured the same for himself. "Yours?"

"Productive."

"Productive how?"

"I put enough shekels together to hire an attorney to draw up a simple will. I'll sign it today after work, then he'll file it at the courthouse."

"Smooth move, Ira."

"That ain't all," he said. "I bought life insurance, naming my brother as trustee if I die before my boys are eighteen."

"Good on you, *amigo*."

Walker looked at Hitchcock. "Your turn."

"I did it—I proposed to Allie."

"And...?"

"The date is February twentieth. You're best man, Sherman and Otis are groomsmen."

"Congratulations. The twentieth is a little over two weeks from now. What's the hurry?"

"Strikin' while the iron's hot."

"She's not...I mean, you know?"

Hitchcock grinned and shook his head. "Nope. She's making me wait!"

† † †

DETAILS OF THE Safeway robbery were discussed at Patrol and Traffic shift briefings, with emphasis on tactics, and 'what if' scenarios.

Captain Delstra used the brazen robbery to demand the City provide a shooting range, pointing out the liability the City faces when none of the sworn officers have trained or qualified with a firearm in four years and counting.

Detectives teamed up to find the two robbers. Leads were few. There were no in-store cameras, and the suspects wore gloves. After getting composite sketches of the suspects from each witness, they sent out bulletins and teletypes and watched for similar cases across the country. No new leads developed. The case was about to be put on inactive status when they got a break.

It came when Hitchcock met Walker car-to-car.

"Might be nothing, Ira, but I remember one employee who didn't seem very nervous about the robbery. He barely answered our questions. You took his statement."

"I remember him, he did seem too calm," Walker said as he dug into his briefcase for his notes "Here it is... Rudolph Sturridge. 3/10/40. Address in Burien area of south Seattle. Washington driver's license."

Hitchcock gave the information to Records. In two hours, Patty had results. "Rudolph M. Sturridge, with this date of birth died a year ago in a car accident," she said.

"Are you sure? He showed Walker a Washington driver's license, and I assume the detectives too."

Patty handed him a news clipping. "Here's his obituary in *The Seattle Times*, with his photograph," she said. "Killed by a drunk driver. I remember it was on the news. The store employee could be anybody—Washington driver's licenses still don't have photographs."

The man in the obituary photograph was not the employee Hitchcock saw at the scene. He showed it to store manager Scott Dawson.

"I hired Mr. Sturridge two weeks before the robbery," Dawson said. "I thought he didn't show up the next day out of fear. Rudy...I mean Sturridge, never called or came in for his paycheck, which I thought was strange."

"Did you try calling him?"

"Phone disconnected. The paycheck we mailed to his address came back unopened."

Hitchcock showed Dawson the newspaper obituary photo of the real Rudy Sturridge. "Is that him?"

A look of shock came over Dawson. "N-no, not at all." He looked at Hitchcock. "So, who did we hire, Officer Hitchcock?"

STURRIDGE'S ADDRESS WAS in South Seattle's Burien area. Hitchcock and Walker went there off duty.

The house was a '50s vintage two-story red brick house set in a hillside neighborhood. It had a sweeping view of Puget Sound. Bedsheets covered all the windows.

The three beater cars in the driveway wore expired license plates.

The hood of an oxidized white '60s Oldsmobile station-wagon parked on the street in front of the house felt warm to the touch. The license plates were expired.

"Red flags everywhere, Roger," Walker said.

"Could this be the suspects' car we saw leaving as we arrived?"

Walker shrugged. "All we saw were tail-lights that

looked like a General Motors car."

No one answered the door.

Walker wrote down the plate numbers and descriptions of the other cars.

Hitchcock sent the information to Detective Sergeant Jurgens, who put Detectives Meyn and Small back on the case. He knew the detectives were too overworked to devote the time necessary to identify, let alone catch the gang of three. He gave the license plate numbers of the cars parked outside to Patty to run for the owner histories of each vehicle. Having registered owner information on the other cars, he drove back to the address, after dark.

The lights in the house were out.

Only the Oldsmobile station wagon was gone.

He drove away for a block, then cut his headlights. He waited a minute, then, seeing no one around, he walked back, flashlight in hand, and opened the mailbox. It was full. He wrote down who each piece of mail was addressed to, and who it was from. He sent the names to Patty for follow-up.

CHAPTER TWENTY-EIGHT
The White Tiara

A Week Later
Renton Assembly of God Church
Renton, Washington

WITH ORGAN MUSIC playing in the background, Walker straightened Hitchcock's tie. They were in the dressing room. "You're smiling too much, Roger. Think about the freedoms you're giving up. Remember your motto, 'All those women, so little time.' Us married guys lived vicariously through your adventures. You're taking all that away from us by biting the dust."

"He's not listening. Hey, kid, stop smiling!" Otis ordered, waving his hand across Hitchcock's face.

"He's a goner" Otis said. "Let's go before they start without us."

"Eat your hearts out, boys," Hitchcock finally said.

"What do you *think* we've been doing?" Sherman kidded.

Heads turned and ladies gasped when Allie appeared at the organist's opening notes of the wedding march, *Here Comes the Bride*. Radiant in her white gown and tiara, her sister-in-law as maid of honor, her oldest brother walked her down the aisle, her eight-year-old niece, dressed in white, scattered flowers before the bride.

Hitchcock waited at the altar, lost in a euphoric state with Walker next to him as best man, Otis and Sherman as groomsmen. Guests included Hitchcock's mother, sisters and brother-in-law in the front row, joined by Doc and Ethel Henderson. Across the aisle sat Allie's mother, her two brothers and their wives and six nieces and nephews. Behind them, on both sides of the aisle, sat Sergeants Breen and Baxter with their wives, two members of Hitchcock's former boxing team with their families and many of the Pancake Corral crew.

Holding an open black Bible. the black-suited preacher read wedding charges and responsibilities to each before he asked, "Roger, do you take this woman to be your lawfully wedded wife; to have and to hold, to love, honor and cherish as long as you both shall live, until death do you part?"

"I do," he replied, his eyes on Allie.

Turning to Allie, the preacher said, "Allison, "Do you take this man to be your lawfully wedded husband; to have and to hold, to love and honor and cherish as long as you both shall live, until death do you part?"

"Yes! Yes! Yes!" she exclaimed, bringing forth a

burst of laughter from everyone.

He would have taken her away as soon as the preacher pronounced them husband and wife, but social obligations being what they are, he waited.

Myrna held Allie in her arms. "Get busy! Sons, Allie, sons!" she whispered, choking with emotion, wiping her tears.

"Welcome to the family. Allie," Hitchcock's twin sisters, Jean and Joan, said, smiles beaming.

† † †

IN THE GRAVEL parking lot across the street, a middle-aged man smoking a cigarette in a tan early '60s Ford pickup watched Hitchcock and Allie come out of the church, smiling and waving at the cheering crowd, brushing rice from their hair and clothes as they got into a gray Wagoneer, packed with camping gear and JUST MARRIED written in soap on the back window, strings of empty cans tied to the rear bumper.

He lagged behind the guests, following them for blocks, honking their horns. After the guests dropped away, the man continued following the happy couple, keeping a discreet distance. He watched Hitchcock stop to remove the cans from the rear bumper and followed them to the beginning of the gravel load that led to Hitchcock's cabana and stopped. Watching the gray Wagoneer disappear into the cedars at the other end of the road, the man lit a Marlboro cigarette and drove away.

CHAPTER TWENTY-NINE
And The Two Shall Become One

THEY FED JAMIE, changed into jeans, boots and warm clothes, except for Allie keeping the tiara on her head.

"What about Jamie, honey?" she asked as she grabbed her luggage.

"Doc and Ethel came back just for our wedding. They said they'd take care of him until we get back."

She stood next to Hitchcock as if her hips were welded to his as they left the cabana.

Returning to their secret wilderness spa, they came to the edge of the steaming mystical waters in the cave. Moments later Allie stood, nothing on but the white tiara on her head, her hair draped over her shoulders like a golden mane, waiting, burning with desire, her voice husky and intense.

"The waiting is over. Take me now, O my man, and make us one."

Her white tiara remained on her when they came together for the first time. Words were inadequate and unnecessary. A driving hunger, long delayed, slaked at last, set up and sealed forever their oneness, creating a new person, one person, one mind, one heart of the two, never to be separate. With each round of passion came a satisfying culmination, followed by another.

After a long night of merging into one, they slept their way into a new dawn, their dawn, until their first sunrise together awakened them. They kissed, and talked delightedly of how many kids they would have, how soon, whether they could afford for her to stop working, and on and on.

They breakfasted in the town of North Bend. An older couple across the aisle glanced at them several times, smiling at Allie, still wearing her tiara like a crown. The man approached as he and his wife got up to leave.

"Pardon us, but by any chance did you two just get married?" he inquired.

"Yes, sir, we got married yesterday," Hitchcock replied.

"We thought so. Your bride is glowing so much it couldn't be anything else. Congratulations," the man said. He turned to the waitress, "Give me their bill, miss. I'm buying their first breakfast as man and wife."

† † †

FROM NORTH BEND, Hitchcock drove northeast into the countryside.

"Where are we going, husband?"

"I have another surprise for you."

After a few minutes he pulled to the side of the road. On the other side of barbwire fence was a large grassy meadow.

"Here we are," he said as he opened the door for her.

"What's this?"

"Walk with me," he invited, stepping between strands of barbwire fence. He led Allie by the hand across the meadow to a natural pond, beyond which stood acres of alders, cedars and fir trees on level land.

"Well, what do you think?"

"Nice land, hon, but..."

"This is *our* land, Baby," he said. "Twenty acres, level, with grass, trees and water. I bought it while I was in college, and finished paying for it out of my inheritance from my father's estate when I came back. We own it free and clear."

Allie nodded her approval as she searched for the best spot to build their home. "What a wonderful place to raise our family. I see us here with kids, dogs and horses, maybe chickens, too."

WHERE THEY WENT for the rest of their two-week honeymoon stayed a romantic secret they would take to their graves. They stayed at her apartment when they returned, while he fixed up his cabana-cave with area rugs and carpet over thick pads atop the linoleum floor.

He covered the brick fireplace hearth with padding and child-proofed the kitchen and bathroom cabinets with locks on the doors.

He hired an attorney to draw up a simple will, naming Allie as his heir, and bought a life insurance policy, naming her as beneficiary. The knowledge that should he die now, Allie would be taken care of, gave him a peace he never knew before.

The incoming tide of changes in his life came in a short time, as if an unseen hand removed the women who didn't belong in his life until only the right one remained.

He had never been a praying man, but he believed in God. He didn't know how to begin, but he felt that to pray the best he could was only right. "Thank you, God, for all this. If this is what You are like, I want more."

Life was good—he wished things would stay as perfect as they are now, but he sensed changes were coming,

CHAPTER THIRTY
Walker and the Dead Cat Caper

WALKER HANDLED EASTGATE for the two weeks Hitchcock was away on honeymoon. Early one morning, after a night of freezing temperatures, he noticed a green unoccupied Ford Taurus behind The Great Wall. He hadn't seen it there before. It was registered to a couple in Seattle. Suspicious of anything to do with Juju's place, Walker kept an eye on it from a distance, sipping 7-11 store coffee to keep warm.

An hour later a Chinese girl he recognized as a waitress arrived in a brown Mercury sedan. She kissed her passenger as he got out of her car and left. The clean-cut, boyish white male in a rumpled suit fished a key from his pocket and opened the driver's door of the Taurus. *Aha, a little overnight hanky-panky*, Walker nodded with a wry grin.

THE TAURUS WENT *clunk* when the man tried to start it. The engine couldn't turn over. Walker pulled up. "I got jumper cables if your battery is low."

The man nodded his head in thanks. Walker noted the wedding ring on the man's finger as he pulled the hood latch under the dash. He chuckled when he lifted the hood. The man came over to look.

"The cat crawled into the engine compartment to stay warm during the night." Walker said. "The fan blade killed it when you turned the key."

"I'm really sorry about the cat, officer."

"Don't worry, I'll take care of it," Walker said. "Your fan belt is broken. I'll get a tow truck for ya."

The dead cat's body was warm when Walker removed it. He let the man warm up in the front seat of his cruiser. After the man left with the tow truck, Walker radioed Sherman and Otis to meet him.

"See this dead cat?" he said, mischief in his eyes as he held it up by the tail.

"Umm-hmm," Sherman said, scratching his chin. "I see you got a dead cat there, Ira."

"Elementary, my dear Sherman," Walker said.

"Do I even want to hear what you have in mind, Ira?" Otis asked, lively humor in his eyes.

"I'm taking bets that if we leave the cat by the back door and hide our cars, when the cook arrives to prep food for the lunch crowd, he'll take the cat inside."

Otis and Sherman each put a five-spot into the pool. The word spread throughout the morning shift. By six-thirty every officer including Sergeant Breen and the morning dispatchers placed bets and the pool amounted to sixty-five bucks. Sergeant Breen agreed to hold any but emergency calls for Walker and Sherman until the cook arrived.

Walker placed the dead cat by the back door.

Walker and Sherman hid their black-and-whites hidden behind the construction equipment behind the Great Wall. They shivered as they crouched behind a dump truck until the cook arrived. The cook put his key in the back door, then stopped when he noticed the dead cat.

Looking right and left, the cook grabbed the cat by the tail, went inside and shut the door. Walker keyed his mic: "The cat's in the door!"

Bets were paid before anyone went home.

AT 11:00 A.M. that same morning, Walker watched Lieutenant Bostwick strut into the Great Wall as he had done every day at this time while Hitchcock was out of town.

At the station an hour later, Walker was off duty and headed down the hall when Bostwick ran past him from his office toward the men's' restroom, covering his mouth with his hand, vomit running through his fingers onto his uniform. He collapsed in the hall, doubled over, retching, defecating in his pants. No one in the station could keep a straight face as ambulance attendants strapped him onto a gurney and took him to the ER.

† † †

At shift briefing the next morning, Sergeant Breen bit his lower lip to keep from smiling when he referred to Bostwick's affliction as a "sudden case of food poisoning for which he will be on sick leave for the rest of the week."

"Hey Tom," Walker whispered to Sherman. "Before I call the Health Department so they can ask Bostwick where he ate, wanna bet that Rowlie had a plate of 'meow mein' at Juju's yesterday?"

"I respectfully decline such an unfair wager," said Sherman, snickering.

CHAPTER THIRTY-ONE
A Darkening Turn

WITHOUT A CALENDAR or counting the days, Hitchcock knew the time to return had come.

Messages in his inbox included one from "Rooster," Randy Fowler's code name, another from "Mata," code name for Gayle Warren, still another from "Tony," code name for Wally Evans.

He dreaded calling Gayle. Word of his marriage had surely reached her by now. She would be hurt, but he had no doubt of Allie being the right one.

It was cold and dark outside but dry. A vague sense that something of significance is about to happen began dogging him as he called in service and headed for Eastgate along the winding curves of Richards Road.

He rousted two drunks sleeping in their cars, the first behind The Steakout, the other in the parking lot of the Hilltop. Having cleared these, he met up with Walker.

"You look the happiest I've ever seen you," Walker said as he cranked his window down.

"I married the right girl, and life is wonderful."

"*That's* obvious. You really scored, you sly-devil-dog, you."

"What happened while I was away?"

"Well, let's see…a huge earthquake hit Los Angeles right after your wedding, maybe you're tying the knot is what triggered it."

"What happened *here*?"

"Gas just went over thirty cents a gallon."

"I bought gas on our trip, Ira. Come on."

"All right—the mother of the dead girl, Stacey Brock, committed suicide right after she got out of jail. She left a note alleging a guy named Art got her and her daughter on heroin. Problem is, she didn't state Art's last name or leave any clues as to where we could find him."

"The mom was on heroin, too?" he exclaimed. "I had no idea. Did you?"

"Appearances can be deceiving."

"What did the daughter's autopsy report say?"

"Massive heroin overdose. The lab tech told me she would have passed out before she could give herself that much."

"Murder," Hitchcock concluded, nodding. "How did the mother die?"

"Overdose of prescription sedatives. She left the furnace on high, making the house very warm, which accelerated maggots and putrefaction by the time we found her. Her blackened skin slid off in our hands when we lifted her onto the gurney."

"Glad I wasn't around for that," Hitchcock said.

"What's worse, her cat had been feeding on her face and fingers, right down to the bone. I just about lost my lunch when I helped move the body."

Hitchcock paused. "Other than the mom and daughter deaths, what else went on?"

"Two more girls ran away last week."

He stared hard at Walker, waiting for more. "Both are fifteen, poor students, chronic runaways with histories of drug use," Walker said. "One, Cheryl Collins, is from my district, the other, Holly Goodrich, is from yours."

"Let me guess. They hung out at Robinswood Park."

"Holly Goodrich, yes. The Collins girl, unknown."

"Any guys involved?" Hitchcock asked.

"The word I'm getting on the street is that the Goodrich girl kept company with a guy named Mike, only description is that he's white, with long blond hair. I made a set of their photos and descriptions I got from their families for you."

He studied the photos. "I'll check my sources later today. Anything else?"

"Yeah, ready for this? Forbes voluntarily requested Delstra to let him return to Patrol at once. Delstra granted it. Kinda makes you wonder…"

"No way!" Hitchcock exclaimed. "How did it happen?"

Walker shrugged. "My guess is the boxing 'lesson'

you gave Mark flipped a switch in him. He's a changed man, a pleasure to work with, a real team player. So tell me—what happened in the boxing lesson?"

"Pain is the quickest teacher."

Walker chuckled. "He told me and Otis he took the job in Warrants to save his marriage, but she split anyway."

"He's better off without her. Anything else?"

Walker's face fell. "This one is hard—I mean really hard. You didn't hear this from me, okay?"

Puzzled, Hitchcock shrugged. "Okay," he replied.

"A week after your wedding, the Seattle-First National bank along the frontage road got held up by a tall guy with an athletic build and a small gal as his partner," Walker said. "They had guns, wore ski masks and made the clerks lie face down on the floor. They took their time looting the tills and got away with a *lot* of cash."

"Go on! A bank robbery like that in my district while I'm gone! Didn't the alarm work?"

Walker shook his head. "Seems they knew how to disable it, which got us thinking it must be an inside job. They got away well before the first unit arrived."

"Any more description?"

"The tellers described the woman as petite and that blonde hair stuck out under her mask. The guy kept calling her 'baby.' He kept saying, 'keep your gun on 'em, baby' and 'grab all the money so we don't run out, baby.' She kept saying, 'Okay, honey.'

"That's weird," Hitchcock said, wondering if he'd run across anyone matching the suspects' descriptions.

"Witnesses said they fled the scene in a dark, late-model station wagon with a roof rack," Walker continued. "The dicks dropped the case after they figured the robbers were you and Allie getting more money for your honeymoon because you ran out, but the local papers are doing a series called 'The Case of the Love-Bird Bandits.'" Walker said, as straight faced as he could manage.

"Hahahaha!" Hitchcock laughed. "You fished me in so well I'm buyin' breakfast! Allie's a good cook, but don't you dare tell her I missed Art's Greasy Grub—I mean Burger Bar—while we were on our honeymoon!"

"So, where did you guys go for two weeks?"

"Ah-ah-ah," Hitchcock said with a happy grin, wagging his finger. "Me no tell. Romantic places—secret places only we know about."

† † †

HITCHCOCK PATROLLED ALONG the same isolated road where he discovered a stolen Ford Gran Torino two weeks ago. 118th Avenue SE was a two-lane asphalt ribbon that stretched for miles south of I-90 with trees and railroad tracks on the east side and swampland on the west side that stretched to Lake Washington.

Something guided him to turn right off the road, toward the lake, on an old dirt road which dead-ended after about twenty yards. He stopped at the end, overlooking the slough, or swamp that stretched south under the Highway 10 overpass, and west toward Lake Washington.

"Okay, so why am I here, looking at nothing?" he muttered to himself out loud, as he gazed at the vast expanse of swamp before him.

CHAPTER THIRTY-TWO
The Girl in the Mercer Slough

THE SUN PEEKED in and out of moving clouds as Hitchcock stared out his windshield. Over four hundred yards of marshy bog known as the Mercer Slough lay below and between him and Lake Washington. A flicker of movement in the brush about two hundred yards away caught his eye. Seconds later he spotted movement again in a different place, close to the first. A raccoon, maybe?

Using binoculars, he spotted two coyotes trotting close together, one carrying a large, round object in its mouth. He got out and leaned against the side of his cruiser to steady himself for a better look. When he refocused his binoculars, he saw the coyote had a human head with long hair in its mouth. Knowing news reporters monitor police radio frequencies, he gave only his location to Sergeant Breen.

"DID YOU TRY to go out there?" Sergeant Breen asked when he arrived minutes later.

"It's a swampy bog, Sarge," he replied. "No solid ground, trails from here exist, but Sweyolocken Park on the other side by the freeway entrance is closer to where I saw the coyotes. It's wet, but there are game trails we can follow."

By 10:35 A.M. two detectives, a pathologist from the coroner's office, accompanied by an assistant arrived at Sweyolocken Park. "Where was the coyote you saw?" the pathologist, wearing overalls and rubber boots asked.

"I'll do my best to find it from here," Hitchcock replied as he led the way, followed by Sergeant Breen and the pathology team. Only a few yards in, the firm footing softened to watery goo that almost sucked the shoes off their feet. They found the decomposing, headless body of a teenage girl, jeans, dark green ski parka, hands and feet partly eaten by animal activity.

Frank Kilmer carefully picked his way in to take photographs. Sergeant Jurgens and detectives. Williams and Small arrived.

Hitchcock, Breen and Walker helped free the body from the sucking dark muck. They struggled to stay on their feet as they lugged the gurney to the parking area, where a knot of reporters had gathered.

The body was covered with a sheet and placed in the coroner's station wagon. Breen posted another officer to keep reporters on the other side of the barrier tape.

The team returned to search for the victim's head.

They struggled to walk through foul-smelling swamp water a foot deep or more and gumbo mud without falling or having the muck suck their boots off their feet.

After another hour of hard slogging in the mire they found the head of a teenage girl over a hundred yards south of the body location.

Hitchcock and Walker met at the station.

"Who was she?" Hitchcock asked.

"Holly Goodrich," Walker replied. "From your district."

"Who took the runaway report?"

"I did."

"What did her parents say?"

"Same old story—Dad abandoned the family. Mom told me Holly's behavior changed, her already poor grades dropped even more, and she became distant from her family and friends after she started seeing some older guy named Mike, she met at Robinswood Park."

"Description?"

"The family never met or saw him."

Hitchcock returned to his cruiser, his shoes and pants were caked with foul-smelling mud. Sergeant Breen congratulated him on finding the missing girl, but his assessment of the situation didn't allow for pats on the back. Another runaway girl had been found dead, and like the others, she had been involved with "Mike."

The finding of the body confirmed the sense of doom he felt earlier. He felt a mixture of anger, grief and frustration at not being able to put a stop to Smith's predations. A new, different sense of urgency took its place. Unlike earlier times, this came as an awareness based on logic rather than intuition—unless they find arrest Mike Smith, there will be more young dead bodies.

CHAPTER THIRTY-THREE
Meeting The Ex

HE CAME HOME, his uniform wet, caked with mud, smelling like swamp water. He stripped to his underwear on the patio before he stepped inside.

"How come your pants and boots are so muddy?" Allie asked.

"Searching for evidence in heavy brush."

"Oh. We can take them to the cleaners on our way."

"To what?"

"Trevor's father called this morning. He wanted to know if he could visit Trevor for a while today. He asked me to meet him at Shakey's Pizza downtown on 106th at five."

"What did you tell him?"

"I said yes. I don't want him telling the court I won't let him see his son."

"Fine," Hitchcock said. "He's five months behind in child support. I'm gonna talk to him about that and a few other things. But first, I need to clean up and catch a few winks."

GLENDON MACAULIFFE WAITED alone in a booth inside Shakey's. He was frail, a five-day growth of beard stubble and pimples covered his cheeks, his eyes were beady, his hair was greasy and unkempt, and the cuffs of his scruffy green ski parka were grimy, yet he exuded an attitude of superiority over everybody, as if he was royalty among peasants. He scowled at Allie and wouldn't shake Hitchcock's hand.

"What's the meaning of bringing *him* here?" he asked Allie, ignoring Hitchcock as if he wasn't there.

"Roger is my husband, Glendon. He's also your son's stepdad. You certainly should want to know who your son will be spending so much of his life with, since it won't be you."

Trevor burst into tears when his father stormed out without even looking at him. Allie knelt and put her arms around him.

Hitchcock followed Glendon to his new red Mercedes. He grabbed him by the sleeve of his parka and spun him around. "Got a message for your mommy and daddy, *boy*."

MacAuliffe opened the door of his car, but Hitchcock slammed it shut. He stepped deep into Glendon's space, nose-to-nose. Glendon stood, shaking.

"The message is Allie is my wife now. I know everything about Tobias Olson, the private detective bum they hired to smear Allie. Tell them I talked to

Bruce Sands, the prison slimeball Olson hired to set Allie up. Tell them any more attempts to smear her will result in a lawsuit and publicity, and I have the evidence. Got that, Little Lord Fauntleroy?"

Glendon MacAuliffe froze, too scared to do anything but nod.

"You're a deadbeat," Hitchcock said, stabbing Glendon's chest with his forefinger. "No real man would get five months behind in child support when he has the money."

He kept finger stabbing Glendon. "Ask your mommy and daddy for a bigger allowance to catch up on your support payments, little boy," Hitchcock jeered. "If you aren't caught up two weeks from now, I'm coming after you."

MacAuliffe couldn't control his trembling. He stood, unable to move or speak.

Hitchcock put his palm on Glendon's chest and shoved him against his car. "Run along home now."

Glendon got in his Mercedes and locked the door. "You don't know who you're dealing with! Wait till my father hears about this!" he shouted from the safety of his car. "You're a killer, but my family *knows* how to handle people like *you*!"

"Famous last words," Hitchcock snorted. "Beat it!"

† † †

HE RETURNED TO Allie and Trevor. "Roger, what happened?" Allie asked. "Glendon's never stormed off like this before. You must have frightened him."

Hitchcock knelt to Trevor's level and put his hand on the boy's shoulder. Trevor hugged him. "It's all right, Trevor, I love you and I'm always here for you," he said in a soothing voice. "Would you let me be your dad from now on?"

Trevor nodded and hugged Hitchcock. Allie wept. "Thank you, husband," she said softly.

AS TREVOR NAPPED, Hitchcock sat beside Allie on the couch with a cup of coffee, shaking his head. "I can't figure you being with a waste of skin like that."

"I told you how I met him."

"I gave him a personal message for his parents. It wasn't pretty, and I wasn't polite. Little Lord Fauntleroy's had people kowtowing to him all his life because of who his parents are, until now."

"Did he threaten you?"

"Nah. He's just spouting hot air because he's scared."

"Tread lightly, honey. Enemies of Glendon's family tend to disappear or have accidents. That I learned from others, not them."

He grinned as he put his arm around her waist. "Well then, let's take our last meal at the Pancake Corral. We'll have Bill Chace administer our last rites, then we'll go home and wait for the boogeyman."

She grinned happily and said, "You're too much."

CHAPTER THIRTY-FOUR
The Death Merchants

IN THE SHADOWS of a hangar at the Bellevue Airfield, two men waited in a black Ford Mustang Mach I Cobra Fastback. They were armed, well-dressed, ex-military-types in their early thirties, the driver white, the passenger Asian. Both were clean-shaved and had close-cropped military haircuts. The passenger scanned the Albertson store parking lot across the highway with binoculars, searching for cops, narcs, or the competition.

At 3:36 a.m. they heard the droning of a small plane in the sky above. The passenger checked his watch. "They're early again," he grumbled.

"You'd think they'd get it. They know delivery is to be made only between three forty-five and four, when the cops are changing shift," the driver said.

"Well, they're here now," the passenger shrugged, "and the time is close enough. Let's get it done so we can deliver and get paid," the passenger said.

The driver flashed his headlights twice.

The Piper Cub landed on the runway. The propeller's spinning slowed to a halt. The men from the Mustang approached on foot. The Asian carried a black briefcase in his left hand, keeping his gun hand free. The driver stood; his leather car coat unbuttoned for quick access to his gun.

The pilot and his passenger were not alarmed by the behavior of the 'Mustang Men' as they called them. They expected them to be packing heat under their coats. The pilot carried a nickel-plated Government Model 1911 in a shoulder holster. His passenger carried a 9mm Walther P-38 in a shoulder rig.

The four men faced each other on the tarmac.

The passenger from the Mustang stared at the two men from the plane, keeping his right hand on his belt buckle, close to the Colt Government Model 1911 .45 automatic in a shoulder holster under his leather Italian carcoat. Without taking his eyes off them he knelt and set the black briefcase on the asphalt. He opened it with his left hand, revealing neat bundles of one-hundred-dollar bills, tightly packed.

He stepped back.

The passenger from the plane held an aluminum briefcase in each hand. His facial expression was passive. He watched the men from the Mustang while the pilot knelt and counted the money. When the pilot looked at him and nodded, the plane passenger set the aluminum briefcases down, opened them and stepped back.

The driver from the Mustang tested a random sample of the white powder from each aluminum briefcase with a law enforcement field test kit. He turned to the passenger and nodded as he closed the briefcases.

THE PLANE TAXIED down the runway and ascended into the night. The Mustang sped east on the freeway. A mile later, it took the Newport Way exit, then turned right, up the winding, steep gravel road to a house on the top of Cougar Mountain which featured a sweeping view of Lake Sammamish. The lights were on inside.

IN A ROTTING workers' bunkhouse at the closed Preston Mill, just off the Preston Highway 10 exit, Mike Smith awoke to an itch in his insides that couldn't be scratched. It was late morning. Two other males slept in sleeping bags on the floor. Because Smith had the only gun, a Taurus .38 revolver, he slept on the only bed, with the only girl. He had the last of the heroin, and all of the money.

His cravings were intensifying by the second. He had only enough heroin for one fix. The others would have to suffer when they woke up. Keeping his revolver close, he heated the drug in a spoon and sucked the liquid into a hypodermic needle. Cinching rubber surgical tubing around his arm, he raised a vein. With the injection came relief—euphoria followed.

Refreshed, Smith tiptoed over passed-out bodies to his car and headed west on the freeway. After a stop at a certain restaurant in Eastgate, Smith spent the next few hours making the rounds of Robinswood and Lake Hills parks and the parking lots of Sammamish and Interlake high schools, selling heroin.

Having wads of cash and an ample supply of heroin remaining, he returned to the shack at the Preston Mill for the girl. She awoke and caressed his shoulder as he injected more into her than before, but not too much. Not yet.

CHAPTER THIRTY-FIVE
Shifting Sands

HITCHCOCK PATROLLED EASTGATE irritably. The shift couldn't end soon enough to suit him. The city was as dead. No calls for him or Walker all morning. Even Otis hadn't radioed that he was headed to the station with a prisoner. The strange silence contradicted what he knew was happening

Drug overdose calls were up in Bellevue and Seattle. Randy Fowler reported two men told him that large separate shipments of heroin and cocaine had hit the streets in the past three days. Their names were only street names. It would take time to track down their identities. At least it was a start.

Wally Evans and Randy Fowler could only update him on what they happened to see or hear. He had no qualified informants to deploy. Until the situation changed, he was helpless, up the proverbial creek without a paddle.

He drove by Lake Hills Chevron. Randy wasn't

there. He called Randy's home from a pay phone. No answer. At the station there was a cryptic message in his inbox.

Using his code name of "Tony," Wally had cancelled their meeting, no reason given. Hitchcock felt like a combat soldier with a rifle but no ammunition.

The booking room was empty. He used the phone there where no one could overhear him when he called Records. Patty answered. "Hitchcock here," he said. "I need a list of names and addresses of everyone arrested for drug-related crimes for the past thirty days."

"Got it, Roger," Patty said. "Anything else?"

"Here are the names of two men supposedly in the know regarding hard drugs coming in. These are street names I've never heard of. See what you can find out."

"It'll take a couple days, maybe three."

† † †

THE FOLLOWING DAY he recognized the floral handwriting on an envelope in his inbox. The note inside read:

> *Roger,*
> *Congratulations on your wedding. It was bound to happen. I hear your bride loves you and is very beautiful. I wish you and her all the best.*
> *Your Ardent Admirer,*
> *Eve*

Eve, cosmopolitan Eve. He had lost her too as a

216

source of inside information when he married Allie. Her revelations about the schemes against him by a small group on the top floor of city hall had saved his career twice that he knew of. It was Eve who first warned him *"You've got a bullseye on your back, Roger."*

† † †

OTIS ARRIVED AT the station as Hitchcock unloaded his cruiser. "What's up, Kid? You look like you just lost your best friend."

He shook his head. "Life is good, Joel. Great, in fact, but something bad is headed my way and I don't know what to do."

"Need help?" Otis asked.

"I just might."

† † †

Friday - 3:45 A.M.
Sergeant Breen at the Podium

"THE BLUE-HOODED pervert struck again," Breen said matter-of-factly, as if he had just announced tomorrow's weather forecast. "This time a twenty-year old woman was assaulted at two a.m. in her basement bedroom in Lake Hills. The victim described the suspect as a white male adult, wearing a blue hooded sweatshirt, approximately six feet, athletic build, unknown age due to his face covering. Victim said his voice sounded older, meaning, I suppose, over thirty."

Everyone but Hitchcock chuckled at Breen's humor.

"Suspect gained entry by jimmying open the rear sliding glass door," Breen continued. "The family upstairs never heard a thing. The backyard is fenced, the gate was latched, but not locked. The suspect seemed to know where in the house the victim would be. The race, height and weight and the M.O. match the naked pervert who escaped from Hitchcock last fall."

† † †

SHERMAN APPROACHED HITCHCOCK just before he rolled out of the station. "You predicted right, Roger. He's escalating. He can't stop. I hope we catch him before somebody dies."

Hitchcock left for Eastgate without a word. He felt responsible for the naked prowler's predations on women since his escape.

The Great Wall, Charlie's Place, The Steak Out and The Wagon Wheel were all secure and their parking lots were empty. He ran the plates of cars and trucks at the Eastgate Motel, Kane's Motel and the Hilltop Inn, finding none with warrants.

The indefinable nagging that something *bad* was coming returned.

† † †

HE SNUGGED HIS patrol car next to the closed Dairy Queen, facing the Albertsons store across the freeway. A light-colored sedan of American make arrived in the Albertsons parking lot. He knew the employees' cars. This one wasn't one of them. The headlights went off, but no one got out. Even with binoculars he couldn't see the driver through the windshield at this distance, or read the license number.

It was 5:16 a.m. He waited.

Two cars he recognized as belonging to employees arrived. The drivers paid no attention to the light-colored sedan as they left their cars and headed to the store. *Whoever is in that car is waiting for Gina to show up. This could be the moment I've been waiting for,* he thought.

At 5:36 a.m. the headlights of the light-colored sedan flashed twice when the white Camaro entered the Albertsons parking lot.

The same red-haired woman got out of the white Camaro. She walked toward the light-colored sedan. A white male appearing to be in his thirties, wearing blue jeans and a dark gray ski parka got out of the other car. There appeared to be and exchange of grins and words between them, indicating they knew each other.

The man handed her an off-white carton the size of a shoebox. *She's done business with this guy before,* he concluded as he watched her lift the lid enough to inspect the contents. She gave him an envelope, and put the carton in the trunk of her Camaro. She went in the Albertsons employee entrance.

The sedan entered the eastbound onramp. Intent on getting the license plate number, he put his cruiser in gear, activated his overhead red light, busted the red traffic signal and accelerated hard across the overpass. He entered the other eastbound freeway onramp. A tall delivery truck between him and the suspect vehicle had to stop for traffic. The suspect vehicle entered the freeway.

When at last he entered the freeway, he sped past the delivery truck at Code Two in the passing lane, forcing traffic over. After a mile he reached the stretch of highway called the Issaquah Flats, which allowed a long view ahead. No light-colored sedan in sight. Frustrated, he returned to Eastgate. More store employees were arriving.

He shook his head, realizing he'd been too far away to see the license plate of the sedan, even with binoculars.

AFTER SHIFT, HE changed into civilian clothes and headed in his Wagoneer to the address of the registered owner of the white Camaro in Issaquah. He took Jamie on a leash with him as a cover in case he was noticed.

The house was a '40s-vintage one-story with moldy green wood siding in Issaquah's historic district. Two old beaters were in the gravel driveway. He made two slow passes ten minutes apart, writing down license plate numbers, then parked down the block, facing the house, and waited.

While Hitchcock was on surveillance in Issaquah, two men were visiting his home in the woods.

CHAPTER THIRTY-SIX
Stalking Hitchcock

THE TWO WERE in their early twenties. They came in from Seattle in a decrepit white early '60s Datsun 610 four-door. They rode slowly down the long gravel road to Doc Henderson's place. The passenger, an Asian who kept checking the driving directions on a folded piece of white paper that had been given to him.

They came to the end of the gravel road. There was no place to turn around unless they drove left up the short, winding blacktop driveway. It was lined on both sides by mature cedar trees. They appeared, facing the Henderson house, the carport and adjoining cabana on the other side of the carport. No cars were present.

"This is the place," the driver said.

The passenger glanced in all directions. "*This* is the place?" He asked, incredulous.

"Yep."

"It is too isolated. I don't like it."

"We won't use it. There's no place to hide the car

here and we're too close to the cop station—we'd be caught before we got off the gravel road. I've been shown another approach."

"Show me."

A one-mile series of turns through the Kelsey Creek neighborhood brought them to the end of a dead-end dirt road above the athletic field of Hyak Junior High.

"I'm turned around. Where exactly are we?"

"Follow me," the driver said.

In silence they walked down a wooded trail which led to the back of the cabana where Hitchcock lived. The driveway and carport were still empty. They walked around the cabana and the main house, testing doors and windows. Finding no one home and every door and window secure, they followed the trail back to the car.

"I feel better about it now," the Asian said. "Escape will be easy, and we won't have to pass the police station on our way back."

"We're gonna be there earlier than instructed," the driver said as he took the Lake Hills Connector to the I-405 onramp.

This alerted the Asian. "Why?"

The driver smirked. "Wait till you see the wife."

The Asian shook his head. "The wife is not our purpose. Only him."

A diabolical grin came over the driver's face. "Wait till you see her."

CHAPTER THIRTY-SEVEN
Struggling For Traction

HITCHCOCK WAS STILL in Issaquah when the two men left his cabana in Bellevue. He ducked down in his seat as the white Camaro passed by and parked on the side of the green house on Alder Street. Two scrawny young white males stepped out of the house, nervously looking around. The same woman he saw at Albertsons got out of the Camaro.

She opened the trunk and removed what appeared to be the same package he saw her receive earlier that morning. The three went inside. Ten minutes later, he saw the curtains move in one of the windows. Fearing the people inside might be looking at him, he left.

HE STOPPED AT Charlie's Place on his way home. At the back door he listened to the clink of pool balls and low male voices talking and chuckling as he waited for his eyes to adjust to the low light.

Two rugged young men wearing stained jeans, flannel shirts and work boots were playing pool. A third man, a bald middle-age construction type, stood belly-up to the bar, nursing a schooner of beer, ogling Debbie, who barely tolerated his attention.

"Hi, Roger. I hear ya got hitched. Say it isn't so," she said, ignoring the customer.

He grinned. "News travels fast in Eastgate!"

Debbie pouted, sticking out her lower lip. "Bummer. How come you never gave *me* a chance? I'd a jumped on it."

"You flatter me."

"I'm serious. I kept hoping you'd ask me out, but you never did. But congratulations anyway. I hear your bride's a stone fox. You'll find Wally in his office."

Word travels fast in Eastgate indeed, he thought as he knocked on Wally's office door.

"About time you got back," Wally said.

"Talk to me, big man. I missed our meeting the other day. What's been happening?"

"Sorry. Had to take my oldest daughter to the doctor. Your Mike Smith has been here a couple times with the same two dirt bags. We got their names and dates of birth when I asked for their ID before serving them."

Wally slid a folded piece of paper across his desk.

Hitchcock read the names. "Ever seen either of these guys before?"

"Nope. They impressed me as local kids who are in

over their heads with Smith. Probly 'cause he's got' 'em hooked."

"How did Smith act?"

"Paranoid. He studied everybody as if they were undercover cops. The bulge under his shirt told me he had a gun in a shoulder holster. The other two sat at a different table, joking around but keeping an eye on the boss. Debbie waited on Smith and chatted him up, like you asked."

"And?"

"Said he's from Carnation. The other two flirted with her but she focused on Smith. He didn't take the bait."

He pocketed the note. "Thanks, Wally, this is a huge help."

"Also, word on the street has it that a big load of heroin *and* cocaine came in a few days ago. It's already hitting the streets. That's all I got."

"You've confirmed what I've been told. Thanks for the tip," Hitchcock replied.

† † †

HE SAW GAYLE Warren's white Dodge Dart parked in front of her apartment. He hesitated to approach the door. *I'm a married man now. Going to her door or seeing her alone isn't appropriate. A phone call is the right thing*, he decided.

He called her from the station. Her voice turned cold when she heard him.

"I heard," she said icily. "I don't mind telling you I'm hurt and disappointed that you married someone else."

He was at a loss for words, but not Gayle. "Before I knew you got married," she said, "I found out about Gina, the woman drug pusher."

"Tell me anyway. People—mostly kids, are dying because of her, Gayle."

"Last name is Balzano, B-A-L-Z-A-N-O. She's from the East. New York or New Jersey, not sure which. Lives in Issaquah with her uncle and some cousins. She's selling heroin and cocaine—getting it from out of state. She's selling Ecstasy now too. Gets it from some local people."

He remembered the exchange in the Albertsons parking lot. She paid for a box of something that she put in the trunk of her car.

"How's she getting it?" He asked.

"By car."

"When?"

"About a week ago. Now leave me alone to lick my wounds," she said as she hung up.

He called Patty in Records. "Here's two guys who are running with Mike Smith. Find out everything you can, not just arrests and Field Interview Reports."

"I'll need a few days."

226

CHAPTER THIRTY-EIGHT
Threat Imminent

ALLIE'S GRAY TOYOTA was in the driveway when he returned home. As soon as he let Jamie out of the Wagoneer, he lifted his nose in the air and followed a scent trail toward the back of the main house, hackles up, growling lowly. Hitchcock followed.

"What's up, big fella?"

Jamie sniffed around the doors and windows of the cabana and the bushes behind it.

Allie stepped outside.

"Did someone just leave?" He asked.

"No, but I just got here. Is something wrong?"

"Jamie's picked up a fresh scent trail around our place and Doc's," he replied.

"Uh-oh."

† † †

THE DOORS AND windows of Doc's house and the cabana were secure, no signs of tampering. He followed

227

Jamie through the woods. Fresh tire marks were on the dirt road above the Hyak Junior High athletic field.

"Looks like burglars came through the woods, casing our place and Doc's," he told Allie when he returned. "Their scent trail goes around our place and Doc's house then straight to the junior high on the other side of the woods. I saw the track of two men."

Allie shuddered and rubbed her shoulders. "Gives me the creeps. Now what?"

"I'll phone in a report and put our place on a daytime patrol watch. Once Doc and Ethel return, the threat will be over because they're home all day."

"Do you think they'll come back?"

He shrugged and shook his head. "*Something* is wrong. Why didn't they hit either place when no one was home?"

"Maybe they're just curious hikers," Allie offered.

"Wandering hikers don't cross the lawn of a strange house then walk around both house and cabana," he said. "They left their vehicle at the junior high, walked the trail to here and then back again—all in a straight line. They weren't wandering or exploring, they came here for a purpose. The intention wasn't burglary because they didn't break in when they could have…"

"So what does that leave?" Allie asked, her tone nervous.

"Us," he replied after a thoughtful pause.

CHAPTER THIRTY-NINE
Tracking the Pied Piper

A WEEK CAME and went. Hitchcock kept an eye out for anyone following or watching him. Patty in Records advised that the two men with Mike Smith at Charlie's Place, Forrest Anderson, 24 and Noah Shapiro, 25 had records going back to their early teens.

Hitchcock read their rap sheets.

As adults they had been arrested together many times by the Seattle Police or the King County Sheriff's Office for drug possession with intent to sell, theft, trafficking in stolen property, and residential burglary. Each had outstanding arrest warrants for controlled substance, theft, and traffic-related charges.

The warrants for Noah Shapiro would never be served. Hikers found his body in the woods of East King County near Carnation five days ago. Like the others, the cause of death was heroin overdose, ruled as accidental. Hitchcock knew it was murder.

Forrest Anderson was at large.

† † †

AS THE RADIO was quiet, Hitchcock snuck out of his district. He knocked on the door of Noah Shapiro's parents' home a few blocks south of the city limits.

No answer.

He went to Forrest Anderson's parents' home a few blocks away. It was a new, upscale split-level house with typical Northwest huge windows to let in more daylight, and custom landscaping.

A trim woman in her early fifties, salt-and-pepper hair perfectly coiffed, dressed in a pleated knee-length gray and white plaid skirt and solid gray sweater, answered the door.

"Mrs. Anderson?"

She nodded, nervous at the sight of his uniform.

"I'm Officer Hitchcock. I came to ask you a couple questions about your son, Forrest, if it's all right."

She looked at his badge and uniform, then at the black-and-white cruiser in her driveway. "You're outside your jurisdiction, officer, but do come in," she said, stepping back, her hand gesturing toward the living room.

He followed her in, taking in the two skylights in the vaulted ceiling, the brick fireplace painted the same white as the walls, glass coffee and matching side tables, the cold stiffness of the ultra-modern furniture. The light gray leather couch he sat on felt as uncomfortable as it looked. She sat across the room from him on a matching armchair, knees together, hands folded on her lap, waiting.

"We have an ongoing investigation of a drug dealer known as Mike Smith," he began. "Your son was seen with him and Noah Shapiro in a bar in Eastgate about two weeks ago. Do you know or ever meet Mike Smith?"

Her expression softened. Her eyes revealed years of heartache as she replied, "Forrest hasn't lived with us for the last four years, officer. He's been a street person since my husband and I made him move out. I can't say I ever heard of Mike Smith, and I doubt my husband has either."

"Do you know how to reach Forrest?"

"Not in a long time. We were wondering if he is all right. When I saw your uniform, I feared you came to tell me bad news. At least now we know he's alive."

"What about Noah Shapiro?"

"Forrest grew up with Noah. They went to the same schools, both of them always in trouble. Stealing, drugs, bad grades. Noah, at least, graduated from Newport High School. Forrest dropped out in his junior year. I hear Noah is dead."

"Yes, he is. When did you last see or hear from your son, ma'am?"

She paused to reflect. "He stopped by, asking for money a little over a year ago. He became angry and left when my husband refused. Sorry I'm not much help."

"Was he with anyone?"

She shook her head.

"Did he come in a vehicle?"

"A Mustang, late model, loud pipes," she replied.

"Color?"

"Dark—black, maybe. It offended us that he would ask for money when he had a car like that."

"It would offend me too," Hitchcock acknowledged. "Smith is turning young people into heroin addicts. Several people who ran with him have died of overdose under suspicious circumstances. Perhaps you might know some of your son's friends who know something that would help us find Smith."

"Forrest's friends are criminals. They never came around here. My husband wouldn't allow it. I know Forrest is still in communication with his two sisters. They live in other states. I'll ask them if they know any of Forrest's friends, and get back to you either way."

He handed her a business card. He stopped again at the Shapiro residence. Still no answer at the door. He left his business card and a note requesting contact.

Patty's report on Forrest was in his inbox. Of the four pages of Field Interview Reports, the latest was over a year old. The people with Forrest then were two men and a girl. The men had outstanding felony warrants. Not surprisingly, the parents of the girl reported her missing over a year ago.

The growing list of dead bodies behind Mike Smith worried Hitchcock. *No doubt this girl is dead, too. It's a county case. The body hasn't been found, maybe it never will be. How many more are there we don't know about?*

† † †

A QUESTIONABLE ACTIONS call at the Newport Marina came in as soon as he returned to Eastgate. He contacted the manager, Wilbur Jenkins.

"The wife and I've been watching this for weeks now, Officer Hitchcock," Jenkins said. "The guy living aboard The Lusty Lady, the forty-foot sailboat moored at the second dock, has people stopping by for only a few minutes, around the clock. This is winter. Should be quiet here till spring."

"Who is this guy?"

"Name's Blake Connors. Claims he lost his job and his house in the first Boeing crash."

"What does he drive?"

Jenkins pointed to the parking lot. "The big silver Mercedes right there."

Hitchcock noted the plate number. "Have you noticed a pattern in the traffic that comes and goes from Connors's boat, Mr. Jenkins?"

"You bet I have. After either of two cars have been here, people come by in droves. About a week later, the flow of visitors slows to a trickle. Then, last week, the volume of cars coming to his boat started up again."

"What kind of people come by?"

"Well-heeled business types in high-end cars," Jenkins said. "It's always after two cars show up, driven by people I wouldn't want to meet in a dark alley."

"Can you describe the two cars?"

"A full size dark gray Jaguar sedan, not new. The

other is a new American hot-rod, green, loud pipes, big emblem on the hood. Young guy with long blond hair drives it."

"Could the green car be a Pontiac Firebird?"

Jenkins snapped his fingers. "That's it," he said. "Shows up in the late morning. After that, cars come by at all hours."

"We've been looking for the driver of that car for some time. If he comes around again, call police emergency, ask for me and do nothing else. He's dangerous. Here's my card. Call this number."

"I'll be more than glad to help you get all the bastards," Jenkins said, his voice stern.

† † †

HE NOTICED A brown paper sack filled with canned food on the kitchen counter when he came home. He asked Allie about it when she came home from work.

"It's for the church food bank," she explained.

"Food bank?"

"A lot of people are out of work and losing everything. They say there's no end in sight of the layoffs," she replied. "I want to do my part. The church I've started attending has a list of desperate families."

"What church is this?" He wanted to know.

"Neighborhood Church. It's halfway from here to Crossroads."

"I know where it is."

"More people are becoming desperate," she said.

"I'm seeing it at work," he said.

"It could be us if you didn't have a government job and some seniority, honey."

"Don't I know it. People are ditching their new cars and reporting them stolen for the insurance money, filing false theft reports, committing suicide, shoplifting food. Reminds me of my parents' stories of the Depression."

"Speaking of work, how was work today?" she asked.

"Exceptional," he said. "More information on this drug dealer we're trying to catch came in. I think we're close to arresting him. The prosecutor's office gave us the green light to pick him up for investigation of homicide."

"Congratulations. I know you and Ira have been hunting this guy for a long time."

"We haven't caught him yet. He's still out there, dealing poison and killing people. Enough about me. How was your day?"

"Busy. Bill hired a new waitress. She started today, a gal who just got out of prison."

"Really? I'm surprised," he said.

"I'm proud of him for giving someone a second chance who is honest about her past."

"This isn't her second chance if she's been in prison in Washington. Only the hardest female cases get sent up in this state."

"She's a little rough, I admit, but she's pleasant and

she seemed to take to me right away."

"What was she in prison for?"

"She didn't say, and of course I didn't ask. Her name is June."

CHAPTER FORTY
A Blue, Blue Morning

TRUE COPS ARE defined by what they do when the work is slow. Like during the early hours, when the radio is quiet, the streets are empty, and it seems there is nothing to do until the city wakes up.

Average officers meet for coffee and wait for the streets to fill and the calls to come in. Those who are truly called to be cops use the wee hours to look under proverbial rocks and bushes to find undiscovered trouble and misdeeds.

Like most true policemen, Clive Brooks disdained the predictability of civilian life. For him, working at a desk would be like living in a cocoon, like being packed in cotton, like kissing your girl through a screen door. If real trouble wasn't to be found, discovering unusual and unique situations would do just as well.

On the belief that dark deeds are always afoot somewhere, Brooks prowled and probed the darkest and loneliest corners of his beat during the quiet times, like a hound padding along a wooded game trail, nose to the ground.

In so doing this morning, he spotted the headlights of a new black Jaguar XJ6 sedan, engine running, headlights aimed broadside at the driver's side of a red Mercury Cougar in the parking lot of the Gas Lamp, a secluded downtown bar located below and out of sight of Main Street.

The middle-aged woman there was quite a sight. In a blue bathrobe and slippers, her hair in curlers, she was bent over, letting the air out of the left front tire of the Mercury. She didn't turn around or stop when Brooks arrived.

"What's the situation here, ma'am?"

"My no-good husband is cheating on me again, officer," she said as the last hiss of air left the last tire. "He told me he was going bowling with his buddies last night. Never came home. He's so stupid he forgot his bowling ball. Found his car here, where I expected it to be."

To make sure a dead body wasn't inside, Brooks shone his flashlight into the interior. "How do you know he isn't sick or in the hospital?" he asked.

"Nah," she scoffed, "his current girlfriend's a cocktail waitress here, another peroxide chippie."

"Is this your husband's car?"

"It's *my* car, registered to *me*. I bought it for him. I earn the money, he plays around. Rodney and work are like oil and water."

She handed Brooks her driver's license. "Check me out. You guys have been to my house several times, always regarding Rodney."

Brooks wondered why she tolerated a cheating husband as he ran her for warrants, previous contacts and car registration. Records confirmed she had been the complainant several times on disturbance calls involving her husband. The Mercury was registered to her only. Her husband's history included two DWI arrests and several contacts last summer for being on foot in a neighborhood late at night, plus traffic citations. His driver's license was suspended.

"Okay, Mrs. Thorndyke. Everything checks clear. Sorry about your situation. I'm concerned your husband might get violent when he sees this. Records tells me we've been to your house for disturbances before. I don't see why–" Brooks stopped himself as he handed her license back to her.

"You were about to ask why I stick with Rodney, Officer Brooks?"

Hooking his thumbs under his gun belt, he nodded.

"As you can see, I am a plain woman. I am not blessed with the attributes most men want in a woman. But God gave me a brain. I went through high school and college without being asked out even once. Because I had no social life to distract me, I have employees working for me and my house and cars are paid off."

Brooks nodded and smiled. "Good on you, ma'am."

"Rodney is a handsome, uneducated playboy who

can't support himself. Champagne taste on a beer budget. I know he married me for my money and he knows I married him to have a man. He's cheated on me from the start, but he's all the man I have or will ever have."

"There's a lot of fish in the sea, ma'am," Brooks countered with raised eyebrows and a nod, but not daring to wink.

"One day he'll leave the bar flies and content himself to be mine."

Without thinking Brooks openly looked her up and down. He smiled his approval with a quick nod. *She's up there in years, but doesn't look bad at all. Pretty decent, actually,* was his assessment. She, he could tell, seemed to revel in his checking her out.

"Where is Rodney now, Mrs. Thorndyke?"

"Don't worry. I fixed her tires, too."

Brooks stifled a chuckle and rubbed his ear. "I'm hard of hearing this morning. Guess I better make sure you get home safely. I'll follow you, if you don't mind."

She smiled at him. "That would be gallant of you, officer."

"Clive," he cordially corrected.

"Dorothy. Call me Dottie," she said with an inviting smile.

"Okay, Dottie, let's get you home."

"Follow me, Clive."

ON COUGAR MOUNTAIN, the room Lieutenant Bostwick was in was totally dark. His head hurt. As his mind cleared, he realized he was on his back, buck naked, lying on silk sheets. He was unsure of where he was. *Silk sheets! Of course!* He reached across the bed with his left arm and felt a woman there—*Juju, of course, Juju—I am at her place,* he thought, relieved at first, but he couldn't remember how he wound up in her bed. In fact, he remembered nothing about last night.

Juju's house was quiet. The luminous dial on his watch read 4:50 a.m. Time to get dressed. For some reason he couldn't move his legs. He couldn't turn over or raise his head. He reached over for Juju lying next to him, but now that side of the bed was empty. *Did she leave? Was she here?* Looking up into total darkness and feeling helpless, he slipped into unconsciousness again.

† † †

WALKER SPOTTED A turquoise and white '55 Chevy Bel Air two-door with baby-moon hubcaps parked in front of the Stereo Center in the Lake Hills Shopping Center. He felt the hood—still warm. Oddly, the interior was filled with rolled up newspaper.

"I'm up here, Officer Walker," a voice called. Walker looked up.

Nick Diafos, a teenager whose family he knew, was on the roof, rearranging the sign letters for the Stereo Center. The word "stereo" had been removed, and the word "for" followed the word "Center."

"Nick? What are you doing up there?"

Diafos, a classically handsome kid of Greek descent, who dated only the best-looking girls, lived on Walker's beat. Walker knew him as president of the senior class at Sammamish High School. Nick smiled sheepishly. "I got off work at the Blue Dolphin downtown at almost four. My buddy Gary Zerr filled my car with newspaper while I was working. This is his dad's business, so I'm getting even."

He realized Nick was rearranging the lettering to read something entirely different. The letters in his hand were A and E. The next letter would be X.

"Don't fall, Nick. First aid isn't my strong suit."

Nick smiled and waved.

† † †

ACROSS LAKE HILLS Boulevard, listening to and watching between wood slats of a backyard fence Walker's exchange with a kid on a roof was the original blue-hooded sweatshirt predator. He waited a minute after Walker drove away, noting the direction of travel.

When Walker didn't return, he approached the house, slim-jim in hand. He slipped the lock on the sliding glass door of the daylight basement and crept toward the downstairs bedroom, where his next victim slept.

He heard the phone upstairs ring as he was about to cover the sleeping victim's mouth with his hand. A male voice answered on the second ring. The man upstairs said, "Yes—this is terrible—I am so sorry. I'll go down and wake her up right away." The phone upstairs was hung up with a clang, followed by muffled sounds of conversation between the man and a woman. The staircase light came on.

The predator dashed out of the daylight basement, raced across the back yard and vaulted to the top of the fence and stopped. He looked back at the house before he dropped onto the sidewalk on Lake Hills Boulevard. A two-year old boy in pajamas was standing in a second-floor window, sucking his thumb, watching him.

He dropped to the sidewalk below, shed his blue hooded sweatshirt, tucked it under his arm, and strolled the two blocks back to his car, hoping no one else in the house he left saw or heard him. It didn't matter if they did—he had seen his victim, asleep, waiting for him.

He had miscalculated his timing, but he would be back—twice over, to make up for this morning's mistake. Waiting until he could collect his due satisfaction from her would be torturous, for she was young and a beauty.

IN BUNGALOW NUMBER 6 of the '40s vintage Bellevue Motel, a mile north of the downtown core, the young man with the new Rolex watch his parents gave him slid out from under the bed. The couple in the bed rented had rented the room after the bars closed at 2:00 a.m.

They slept as he scribbled a note and left it on the desk, giving their intimate performance a C Minus and thanking them for the entertainment. He took their clothes and car keys and threw them into the brush. He urinated on their clothes, then hid to watch the police respond.

LIEUTENANT BOSTWICK AWAKENED again. The gray predawn light enabled a view of Lake Sammamish. He staggered into Juju's kitchen. He didn't remember getting dressed. Maybe someone dressed him. His white undershirt was missing. His blue uniform shirt was unbuttoned and untucked in. His gun belt was slung over his shoulder, he stepped on his untied shoelaces. Juju was not around. He left in the black detective car he took without authorization.

Knowing he would have to pass through Eastgate where Hitchcock was working, Bostwick took Newport Way as the back route to Interstate 405 to get to Medina instead of taking Highway 10.

He had never felt like this before—groggy—drugged. There was no traffic as he cruised along two-lane Newport Way. He dozed off, then a jolt and a crash awakened him. He stopped. He had side-swiped a Ford Country Squire station wagon parked on the street. The crash was loud enough to awaken neighbors. He looked all around. Seeing no witnesses, Bostwick fled the scene.

THE FEW CARS passing through Eastgate early on Sunday mornings were hunters, fishermen, straying spouses sneaking back home, or churchgoers. Hitchcock cited the driver of a tan Rambler sedan on Newport Way after he paced it at fifty in a twenty-five zone for three blocks.

A well-dressed middle-aged couple was in the car. The driver was thin, wearing a gray suit and plaid necktie, a small gray brim dress hat and glasses. He rolled down the window.

"Good morning, sir. I stopped you for speeding. I clocked you at fifty for two blocks. The sign you passed states the speed limit is twenty-five."

"I know, I know," the man grumbled. "Don't you have anything better to do? Can't you see we're on our way to *church*? Why aren't you catching burglars and arresting hippies instead of harassing us?"

He returned to the driver, citation in hand. "Sign at the line marked X, please."

The driver signed.

The couple kept the speed at exactly twenty-five the rest of the way to church. When the Rambler turned into the parking lot, the man rolled his window down, stuck his arm out and shook his fist at Hitchcock, who beeped his horn three times and waved.

† † †

HITCHCOCK U-TURNED on Newport Way. Facing him on the other side of the four-way intersection above

Eastgate was an unmarked police car, a black Ford Fairlane, the license plate of which was of his department. The driver ducked down as he passed by. The car then sped across the intersection.

Suspecting a city car had been stolen, he U-turned, flipped on his emergency red light and keyed his mic: *One-Zero-Six, Radio, stopping am unmarked Department vehicle, bearing Washington plate David 63789, operated by unknown subject on westbound Newport Way at 152nd Avenue SE.*

He unsnapped his holster as he approached. None other than Lieutenant Bostwick exited the city car, sunglasses askew, uniform shirt unbuttoned, his bare stomach bugling, no pants belt or gun belt, his face red, angry and contorted. He couldn't see the damage to the right side of the detective car.

Stunned, Hitchcock asked, "Uh, Lieutenant?"

"Shut up Hitchcock! Get back on patrol! You've no business stopping me!" Bostwick shouted, waving his arms.

Hitchcock, hands on his hips, stared at Bostwick for long seconds. "Very well, Lieutenant, let's be on our way then," he said. "Of course, I'll write a report."

Bostwick's eyes bulged as he shook his finger at him but said nothing as he got in the car and drove away.

CHAPTER FORTY-ONE
The Spy from Purdy

PRETENDING TO BE asleep on the couch when Allie came home from work, Hitchcock reached for her arm when she came close to him. She brushed his hand away. "Stop, honey, I want to talk."

"Okay, so do I," he said as he sat up. "You first."

She snickered as she sat on the bed. "You can't fool me. You don't want talk."

"You're right—I don't. You know what I want," he said, reaching for her again.

"Down, boy. I got forty dollars in tips today."

"That's what happens when you're a stone fox in a white dress in a public place. So where are you taking me to dinner?"

She laughed and playfully slapped his shoulder.

"You laugh but something is bothering you," he added.

"You know me that well, don't you? The new waitress, June, somehow knew I'm married to a cop, and

I don't think anyone at work told her."

"Any of the regular customers who know us could have," he said.

"Maybe. But she's been asking me too many questions."

"Like what?"

"Where do I live, who takes care of Trevor when you and I are working, what's it like living with a cop, stuff like that."

"*That's* a red flag," he said, gripping her arm. "Get me her last name and I'll run a check on her."

"How will you know where she did time?"

"There's only one prison for women in Washington—Purdy. Only the hardest cases go there."

"Your turn. How was your day?"

"Well, no one asked me any personal questions. Sundays are either super quiet, or real busy. Except for an unexpected run-in with Lieutenant Bostwick it was quiet the whole shift."

"Bostwick? On a Sunday morning?"

He nodded. "As strange as it was, I still have this feeling that we're being dogged."

"Dogged?"

"Yeah. As in watched-followed. Something big is coming. Tomorrow or the next day. Good it ain't."

"My ex-father-in-law's private detective again?"

He shook his head. "Worse."

CHAPTER FORTY-TWO
The Big Scoop

ACTING ON GUT instinct to go to the rear of the Eastgate Albertsons store right after shift briefing, Hitchcock took a portable radio from the sergeant's office. After a swift sweep of bar, motel and bowling alley parking lots, he met Walker car to car. It was 4:25 a.m.

"What's up?' Walker questioned as he rolled down his window.

"Today's the day."

Walker stared at him, inquiring.

"In a few minutes I'll be in the bushes at the back of Albertsons, close enough to see inside Gina's car when she arrives," Hitchcock said. "I need you in position on the other side of the freeway, out of sight, in case I see her selling dope out of her car again."

"You're done waiting for her to show up with something besides small amounts of grass?"

"I've tolerated her dealing weed right under my

nose long enough. Today's the day. We arrest her, even if it's for only one joint."

"She doesn't arrive this early."

"I got a strong feeling today will be different."

"Okay," Walker said. "I'll hide behind the Dairy Queen, so she won't see my car as she comes up the off ramp. I can cross the overpass quick when you give the signal."

Hitchcock held up the portable radio. "With this I can reach you without having to run to my car."

† † †

AT A POSH all-night restaurant and bar across the street from the Seattle-Tacoma International Airport, Ricky Burns, the young late-shift bar tender, finished his on-the-house breakfast.

He closed the door to the manager's office while he adjusted his shoulder holster and checked his new .357 Magnum. He liked the feel and heft of the big gun under his left arm. Covering it with his Italian leather car coat, he felt like a Mafia enforcer as he opened the trunk of his gleaming new black Dodge Charger.

The briefcase was still there. He double-checked its contents. All the money was there. He headed north on Interstate 5, to eastbound Highway 10 to meet his contact. It was 4:30 a.m.

† † †

AT 4:48 A.M. HITCHCOCK hid his cruiser on the other

side of the church, out of sight, above the Albertsons store. He settled into the scotch broom brush above the parking lot with binoculars and portable radio. He keyed the mic: "Radio check?"

"Loud and clear," Walker replied.

He focused his binoculars on a new black Dodge Charger entering the Albertsons parking lot. It U-turned and parked away from the building, facing the freeway. Its headlights went out.

Hitchcock keyed the mic on his portable as he focused his binoculars on the license plate. "Black Dodge Charger arrived. Adam Zebra Tom Nine Eight Three, Washington."

"10-4, I'll run it," Walker acknowledged.

Another car entered the lot, passed the black Charger and stopped in the Albertsons employee parking area. Two men got out. Hitchcock recognized them as store employees. They entered the back of the store, paying no attention to the black Dodge Charger.

Hitchcock's pulse began racing when the headlights of the Dodge Charger flashed once at Gina Balzano's white Camaro.

He updated Walker as he focused his binoculars on the meeting. "Suspect arrived. Making contact with the black Charger. Drivers are out of their cars. Stand by."

Burns held a slim dark briefcase in his left hand, keeping his "gun hand" free, and his jacket open, the way he read gunmen did in crime novels. He nervously looked around as Gina met him. For long seconds he studied the brush where Hitchcock hid.

A combat veteran and big game hunter, Hitchcock knew that movement catches the eye. He breathed slow, shallow breaths, careful not to even twitch. When he focused his binoculars on Burns's eyes, his heart froze. They were looking at him.

Burns calmly returned his attention to Gina as she handed him a black nylon satchel. He opened the passenger door of his car and leaned inside to inspect the contents.

Hitchcock watched as Burns gave an approving nod to Gina and handed her the briefcase. She opened it on the trunk of her Camaro. Hitchcock's binoculars enabled him to see the briefcase contained stacks of bundled bills. He watched Gina quickly count the money and place the briefcase in the trunk of her car.

Burns got into his car. Hitchcock radioed Walker: "I just witnessed a big transaction. Male suspect in Dodge Charger heading to freeway. Wait until I catch up to you to before you make the stop."

"Charger's on the westbound onramp. I'm on him now," Walker advised.

Hitchcock scrambled to his cruiser the second Gina went inside the store. He activated his emergency light and busted through two red traffic signals then keyed his radio mic: "I saw the female suspect give him a black bag which he put on the front seat. I saw him give her a briefcase full of money. Let's take him before he gets to the 405 Interchange."

Walker radioed Hitchcock: *"Be advised there are four King County Failure To Appear warrants confirmed for Richard Burns, the registered owner."*

Hitchcock caught up to Walker just before the interchange with the 405 freeway. He keyed his mic again: "Now!"

Walker flipped the emergency light switch on his console. The Charger pulled over on the gravel shoulder. Walker unsnapped his holster, opened his driver's door as a shield and remained seated. He keyed his loudspeaker microphone and said, "Driver—turn off your engine. Roll down your window. Put your hands out where I can see them."

† † †

BURNS FIDGETED UNCONTROLLABLY, wondering what he should do. *The satchel!* He cursed himself for putting it on the seat next to him instead of in the trunk. He shoved it off the front passenger seat to the floor. His heart raced like a jackhammer. Being caught with this much heroin meant a lengthy prison sentence. Not delivering it meant death. His cold hand shook as he reached under his leather jacket and gripped the butt of his .357, thinking, *I'll just wound the officer.*

He heard a metallic *click-clack* followed by three metal-on-glass taps on the passenger door window. He turned his head to find himself staring down the gaping barrel of a shotgun. It looked as big as a train tunnel. The officer holding it had his finger on the trigger. Burns's guts turn to water. *I'll be dead any second.* Urine filled his pants as he put both hands outside the driver's side window.

WALKER OPENED THE driver's door and aimed his revolver at Burns's head. "You're under arrest. Hands behind your head. Step out slowly." Walker holstered his gun, handcuffed Burns and removed the revolver from his shoulder holster.

"What did you stop me for, officer?"

"Are you Richard Burns?

He hesitated, then replied, "Yes, sir."

"You have four outstanding warrants for failure to appear in court. Also, your driver's license is suspended."

Burns sighed and shook his head, trembling but trying to play innocent. "That's what I get for being so busy. Any chance I can get a break to take care of those tickets today?"

"Where are you headed, Mr. Burns?"

"Seattle."

"Is that where you live?"

"Yes, sir."

"Where are you coming from so early?"

Unable to come up with a quick sob story, Burns blurted, "Please, officer. I just forgot about those tickets. Let me go. I promise you I'll take care of them today."

Walker handcuffed Burns and removed a slip of paper sticking above his shirt pocket. He put Burns into the back seat of his patrol car.

"Bingo," Walker said, grinning as he handed the slip of paper to Hitchcock. The note bore the full name and home phone number of Gina Balzano.

"I saw him shove the satchel off the passenger seat to the front floor," Hitchcock said. "The heroin is in it. The money he bought it with is in a black briefcase in the trunk of Balzano's Camaro. We need to act fast!"

Walker returned to Burns. "All right, Mr. Burns, we're taking you in on the four warrants. Plus, you're under arrest for Carrying a Concealed Weapon Without a Permit, and Driving While License is Suspended."

Walker advised Burns of his Constitutional rights and asked him if he understood them.

"Yes, I understand, but please don't touch my car. It's brand new. I can have a friend pick it up."

Playing his dumb-cop act, Walker said, "Well, maybe...just maybe we could. It's such a beautiful car."

"Officer, thank you," Burns gushed gratefully. "My best friend can pick it up right away, and I'll gladly go with you guys to get these tickets cleared up."

"Sure thing, Mr. Burns, but I don't want to get into trouble. I better ask my sergeant."

He started to panic. "Oh no, officer. I'll sign a waiver or anything you want."

"That's really thoughtful of you, Mr. Burns, but I just remembered our sergeant is busy on another call. I'll check with my partner."

Walker approached Hitchcock as he inventoried the

trunk of the Dodge Charger. "Roger, I'm playing your guy like a fiddle. He's ready to spill his guts. He's scared we'll find the drugs. I'm acting like I'm on his side, helping him get a friend to pick up his car but you won't go for it. Just keep shaking your head."

Walker hammed it up, making animated pleading motions with his hands and loud comments like "Aw, come on!" and "Have a heart!" Hitchcock kept his back turned to Walker and the suspect, shaking his head, but laughing when Walker stamped his foot and waved his arms for show.

He returned to Burns, throwing his hands up as if exasperated.

"I'm really sorry, Mr. Burns. My doggone partner sure can be hard-nosed at times. He says we can't leave your car on the freeway. Too dangerous. But don't you worry—we'll not only protect your beautiful car, but we'll also inventory the contents right in front of you before we impound it for safe-keeping. Is there anything valuable in your car you want us to know about, Mr. Burns?" Walker asked in his best dumb cop voice.

"Uh, uh, uhhh," Burns groaned.

"No? Well, as a courtesy, we'll let you watch us inventory everything, okay? I'll be right back."

Burns went into convulsions when he saw Hitchcock open the black satchel he received from Gina and hold up two plastic bags of white powder, each weighing about a pound, from the satchel.

Hitchcock saw Burns vomiting on himself and the

back seat of Walker's cruiser. "You're right, Ira," Hitchcock said, snickering. "He *is* spilling his guts! He's *your* prisoner now!"

Walker took Burns to the Overlake ER.

Hitchcock sealed the Charger with evidence tape and impounded it. He took the satchel and Burns's revolver to the detective office.

† † †

THE OVERLAKE HOSPITAL ER docs determined Burns suffered from nothing more serious than anxiety. Walker brought him to the station, placed him in an interrogation room and removed his handcuffs. "Have a seat and relax," he said as he left.

The office narcotics test kit determined the white powder to be pure heroin. Detective Small told the booking officer to not allow Burns to call anyone until further notice. He ran the details past the prosecutor's office, then told Dispatch to have Hitchcock call him.

Small's phone rang in five minutes. He listened, acknowledged that he understood, and met Hitchcock. "The deputy persecutor says to arrest this Gina broad for VUCSA. You and I'll get her, seal her car and have it towed here. Then I get a search warrant," he said.

† † †

MINUTES LATER, LARRY Meyn entered the interrogation room. "I'm Detective Meyn, Ricky," he said, forcing himself to ignore the wrenching smells of vomit and urine on Burns's clothes as he shook hands with him.

"Is it okay to call you Ricky?"

"Why not," Burns said, dejection written all over him

Meyn sat in a chair facing Burns. "Do you understand your rights, Ricky?"

"Yes, sir."

"I want you to read your rights out loud to me from this statement form and sign it that you understand your rights."

Burns read his Miranda Rights out loud from the form and signed.

"Are you okay now? You're not feeling sick anymore?"

"I feel lucky to be alive."

"Lucky to be alive?" Meyn echoed, another of his standard interview and interrogation tactics.

"Yeah. One officer aimed a shotgun at my head," Burns said, fidgeting.

"The officers were being cautious, Ricky. You see, they already knew what you were up to before they pulled you over."

"What do you mean?"

"You've been taken for a fool, Ricky, is what I mean. Before the officers stopped you, you met a girl named Gina in a white Camaro in the parking lot of the Albertsons store."

"I did?" Burns squeaked, panic rising in his voice.

"Gina has red hair. She works at Albertsons. You gave her a black briefcase full of money and she gave you the heroin we took from your car. Over two pounds. You tested it before you gave her the money."

Burns broke out in a fit of nervous coughing.

"There's more, Ricky. We found your drug-test kit in your car. We tested the powder ourselves: positive for heroin. You're being charged with felony drug possession with intent to sell. Got the picture?"

Burns slumped in his chair and stared at the ceiling. "I'm dead," he moaned.

"I'd like to hear your side of the story, Ricky." After a silence of thirty seconds, Meyn put his hand on Burns's shoulder. "As bad as this is, Ricky, as hopeless as it seems, you do have a way out, Ricky."

Burns looked at him, desperate. "How?"

"I see smart young guys like you get themselves in over their heads all the time, Ricky. Often in even worse messes than this. Why, last month we had a guy who was looking at some serious prison time, but by working with us he was able to get a fresh start, and he never went to prison, which is what I am sure you're hoping for, right, Rick?"

Silent, looking down, Burns muttered something.

"Is that a yes?"

"I wouldn't survive prison."

"Ricky, what happened to you is just a case of one bad thing leading to another, and next thing you know, things are out of control. It happens to all of us. Right,

Ricky?" Detective Meyn said as he got out a blank statement form.

"Right," Burns reluctantly agreed.

"Write down everything. Leave nothing out."

CHAPTER FORTY-THREE
Nailing Jezebel

THE STORE MANAGER led Hitchcock and Detective Small to the meat department where they arrested Gina. Her face as Hitchcock handcuffed her revealed bottled rage as fierce as if she had screamed and fought.

They took her out the back door. She stopped in her tracks when she saw a tow truck driver hooking heavy steel cables to the underside of her Camaro.

Hitchcock arrived at the station with Gina in the back seat as a uniformed officer placed Ricky Burns, in handcuffs, in the back seat of a patrol car.

"There goes your partner in crime, Gina. He spilled his guts so now the dicks are getting a search warrant for your car. What will happen to you now that you lost all that money? We got all the heroin you sold Burns too. So, unless you cooperate, you're in for a long-term change of address. You'll need protective custody."

Gina barely held her silence as Hitchcock called in his ending mileage and walked her into the station. Clerks at the public window froze at the sight of a seething, handcuffed woman, blood on her forearms and hands, her white apron caked with blood, smelling of blood and raw meat, fierce, soulless eyes glaring like a caged wild animal at anyone who dared to look at her.

A uniformed police matron strip-searched Gina in the booking room, then escorted her to the interrogation room. The matron stood by as Detective Meyn went in and closed the door.

† † †

DETECTIVE CAPTAIN HOLLAND handed the search warrant affidavits, officer reports, copies of evidence logs, and Burns's signed confession to his secretary.

"Make extra copies of these for the Seattle narcs, and prepare a cover letter stating that both suspects have been booked into jail, and that the male suspect, Burns, has talked. Also mention that the evidence we seized tested positive for heroin. I'll sign it as soon as it's ready. I'm calling SPD, then the prosecutor's office. They'll have to move fast."

From the Chief down to the front desk clerks, the Department was abuzz with the excitement of a record-setting drug seizure with arrests.

† † †

THE NEWS MEDIA followed up with stories based on the Department's carefully worded press releases and the prosecutors' statements of probable cause.

Hitchcock, sensing trouble of another sort was headed his way, turned his attention homeward.

CHAPTER FORTY-FOUR
A Wary Peace

FAMILY LIFE SUITED Hitchcock well. With Allie and Trevor in his life, he had the foundation upon which to build his own family. He meant it to be as idyllic as the family life his father bequeathed to him.

He started Trevor on baseball, playing catch with him in the back yard and under the covered patio when it rained. There were trips with Allie and Trevor snow-sledding on the ski slopes of Snoqualmie Pass, hiking on the steep trails to the top of Mount Si in North Bend, picking berries on the farms open to the public in the Snoqualmie Valley and the Overlake Blueberry Farm next to the Mercer Slough in Bellevue.

On cold rainy evenings, he built a fire in the fireplace after dinner, and read stories to Trevor. At bedtime, he played guitar and the three sang lullabies together.

During one of their trips to their secret wilderness spa, Hitchcock, Allie and Trevor were soaking in the steaming mineral waters where he proposed to Allie, when Jamie emitted a low growl as he stared out the cave entrance.

He and Allie exchanged wary glances as he left the water, revolver in hand, and peered into the forest outside. Jamie remained beside him, growling. After waiting and seeing no one, he approached Allie, who was still in the warm water.

"What do you think that was all about?" she asked.

He shook his head, keeping his eyes on Jamie, who stared at the mouth of the cave, a low growl rumbling in his chest, his coat bristling. "I don't know," he said in a low voice, keeping his eyes on the entrance. "But Jamie doesn't mess around with false alarms. Get dressed. A threat of some kind is out there."

"What could it be, honey?"

"The woods outside are too quiet," he said. "Something or someone's out there, watching us."

They dressed quickly. He put a leash on Jamie and stood at the cave entrance, listening intently. He neither saw nor heard anything, yet goosebumps covered him, and Jamie continued to growl. They crossed the meadow to the Wagoneer.

"Are we okay, honey?" Allie asked.

He shook his head warily as his eyes scanned the tree line and the heavy foliage. "I can't shake the feeling we're being stalked."

She rubbed her arms with her hands. "Is this your sixth sense you told me about?"

"Yep."

"Oh boy," she said, shivering. "How come you don't let Jamie track it down?"

"Because I don't know what 'it' is."

"What do you mean?"

"Animal or human."

"You're not saying you believe in Sasquatch, are you?"

"No. But I know hunters who have been stalked by cougars in these woods, which is why I don't let Jamie loose. He'd be no match for even one cougar," he said.

They came within view of their Wagoneer.

"You'll have to be my eyes as we leave. Driving out of here will demand my full attention. Keep an eye out for another vehicle, hidden or not," he told her.

They rode in silence down the precipitous mountain trail in low gear, Allie looking in all directions. She didn't see another vehicle or person all the way back to the paved road.

"Now that that's over, husband, take me dancing tonight."

He frowned as he steered around a sharp bend in the two-lane road to town. "If my mom will take Trevor tonight, I know just where to go."

CHAPTER FORTY-FIVE
Comes the Stranger

THE HIDEAWAY WAS a rustic country style restaurant and dance place on a gravel lot on the northwest shore of Lake Sammamish. The music tended more toward country, and the mostly blue-collar crowd tended to get rowdy easily.

The country music band drew a large crowd that night. Hitchcock and Allie didn't notice the stocky, nondescript man in his early forties, wearing fake glasses and western clothes, leaning against the wall facing the dance floor, holding a glass of beer.

He was alone, yet his engaging smile and country-boy persona blended with the patrons seamlessly. Because he resembled Gene Autry, the '50s cowboy music and TV star, people warmed to him. He knew country humor, as his quips and jokes proved, and country music too, for he sang along with the lyrics and tapped his feet to the live music as he watched couples dance. With a congenial smile he hoisted his glass as a toast to the better dancers. Between songs he chatted amiably with the men about hunting, guns, trucks, dogs and livestock. With the women he told clean jokes about the trials and tribulations of raising teenagers.

In the middle of the traditional favorite song *Jambalaya*, one couple bumped into another. The men exchanged words, the words became threats, the threats became a shoving match, shoves became punches, then the women joined in the fight, knocking each other into other couples and the fight spread across the dance floor and out into the parking lot.

Hitchcock whisked Allie away as Redmond cops arrived in force. He didn't notice the stocky stranger who also slipped through the crowd to the parking lot.

"Wow, honey, that was exciting but it will be a while before I want to go back."

"Yeah, their food was a bit too salty," Hitchcock quipped as he put the Wagoneer in gear.

"Silly boy!" Allie laughed as she lightly slapped his shoulder.

They didn't notice the headlights of an early '60s Ford pickup following them.

† † †

A COUPLE DAYS later, Allie said, "Honey, The Blue Ridge Mountain Boys are playing at Tom's Teepee this Friday and Saturday. They're from North Carolina. I never thought they'd bring their tour this far west. Can we go, even for a couple hours? I haven't gone clogging since I was a kid."

"Tom's Teepee, the tavern in Bellevue? I didn't know they have live music there. And what's clogging?"

"A folk dance derived from Irish dances to Bluegrass music. The dancer's shoes make music by strikes of the heel and the toe, against the floor in time with the music."

"What about Trevor?"

"My mom already said she'll stay with him so we can go. Please take me."

"Weren't you raised on local rock and roll, same as me, like The Fabulous Wailers and The Sonics?"

"We're originally from North Carolina."

He grinned and nodded. "Of course, we'll go."

"Thank you, hon. Be sure to wear hard-heeled shoes or boots. Making a rhythm with your feet is the thing. I promise you the best time ever."

"Okay, but I can't imagine much of a crowd for Bluegrass music in Bellevue."

"Don't worry. The place will be packed with folks from Seattle and Renton and there's a community of Tarheels in the woods up north of Everett. The place'll be packed, you'll see."

CHAPTER FORTY-SIX
Clogging

MUCH TO HITCHCOCK'S surprise, pickup trucks with rifle racks in the back window filled the parking lot at Tom's Teepee. The only open spot was far in the back.

He wore his old cowboy boots with hard leather soles, a plaid shirt and jeans. Allie wore a white blouse, pleated plaid skirt and hard-soled, laced shoes. Even though the band hadn't started yet, the place was so packed they had to share a table with another couple.

The band leader, a skinny fellow in his late fifties, glasses, white cowboy hat, white long-sleeved western-style shirt, fiddle and bow in hand, stepped up to the microphone. Behind him stood men with a guitar, a banjo, another with a fiddle, and a base fiddle. The blue canvas sign tied to the wall behind them read: THE BLUE RIDGE MOUNTAIN BOYS in white letters.

"Gentlemen, grab yore ladies and make a circle," the leader drawled into the microphone as the players started strumming. Hitchcock and Allie entered the floor with other couples and joined hands with others in a circle.

Fiddle tucked under his chin, bow in hand, the leader counted, "One, two, three," and a fast-paced tune took off.

Dancers stepped into the middle of the circle toward each other, bowed, stepped back, and paired off, the men put their arms around their women's waists, formed a circle facing in one direction, dancing counter-clockwise, heels and toes clicking a percussion rhythm in perfect time to the music. Hitchcock had never seen anything like it.

That clogging is an athletic folk dance impressed him. The basic foot movements involve a two-stage brushing motion of the heel against the floor with one foot, in time with the beat of the music, then back, striking the ball of the foot on the floor, swinging that foot out and across the other leg in a sweeping motion and back, then the other foot doing the same, while the men circle the waists of their women as they dance the same step, snapping their fingers to keep time.

In a few seconds of trying, Hitchcock caught on well enough to keep up with the other dancers. A pre-Civil War tune, *Cotton-Eye Joe* the lead fiddler sang made for thunderous, perfect dance cadence.

Never had Hitchcock enjoyed dancing so much. As the third tune began, the older dancers faced each other in double lines, holding hands lifted high so as to make a tunnel, through which the younger dancers passed and the crowd cheered "*Yeee-oooww!*" in unison each time a couple danced through the tunnel, holding hands, dancing to thunderous music and percussive foot beats. By now the older men stepped out, smiling, panting and pulling handkerchiefs from their back pockets to mop bald sweaty foreheads.

† † †

NEITHER HITCHCOCK NOR Allie noticed the same friendly-looking, stocky Gene Autry lookalike from The Hideaway leaning against a wall, watching them. This night the stranger wore faded blue jeans that had white threads at the cuffs, a jeans jacket, tan felt cowboy hat, scuffed brown cowboy boots. As he did at The Hideaway, he blended right in with the crowd, smiling, greeting people, smoking cigarettes, nursing a beer.

"I'M IMPRESSED THAT you caught on to clogging so fast, honey," Allie happily remarked as they headed home.

"I had the best time ever," he said, smiling as he stopped at a red traffic light. She kissed him hotly until the light turned green.

"It surprises me to see a Bellevue boy who likes country music. How did that happen?" she asked as he drove into the intersection.

"I got exposed to it in the Army through the Southern boys in my unit. Country songs have better messages today than rock. I hate the anti-American lyrics in some of the new songs, like *'American Woman.'* While our guys are still fighting in Vietnam, songs like that trash the country and scorn us who fight. Our parents' generation would never put up with such traitorous trash."

Allie moved across the seat until she was hip-to-hip with him. She took his hand in hers as they entered the beginning of the long gravel driveway to their cabana.

"I want you tonight," she said.

He looked at her, a loving smile on his face, unaware that the headlights in his rearview mirror had followed them from Tom's Teepee.

The tan Ford pickup stopped at the beginning of the long gravel driveway to Doc Henderson's. The driver's smile as he watched Hitchcock's red taillights disappear wasn't the friendly grin he put on for the folks in Tom's Teepee.

CHAPTER FORTY-SEVEN
The Attack

THE VAGUE PREMONITION that had been dogging Hitchcock for days grew in intensity the next morning. The air was cool, dry and breezy as he slogged through his calls, a residential burglary, an adult shoplifter in custody at Eastgate Safeway, two traffic stops, another juvenile runaway report involving a teenage girl.

The foreboding increased as he headed for home.

He arrived at a surprising scene.

Jamie had two strange young men backed up against the brick carport wall, snarling, ears flat, teeth bared, hackles up. The strangers were too frightened to move. *What's this? Who are these guys?*

They were in their twenties, one a sneaky-looking white male, scrawny, long-haired, filthy, acne scarred face with puss-filled pimples. The other was Asian, good looking, tall, fit, clean, short haircut and well dressed. He had a military aspect about him.

"What are you guys doing here?" he demanded.

They reacted strangely to the police uniform under his windbreaker jacket. "We're lost," the white guy said, nervous, his eyes focused on Jamie. "Exploring these woods is all," the Asian, also nervous, said at the same time.

The cabana sliding glass door around the corner opened. Trevor was screaming in the background as Allie yelled out, "They tried to force their way in when they saw me, Roger! I called the station!"

The white suspect made a sudden dash around the corner in Allie's direction, headed for the lawn and the woods beyond. Jamie went after him, lunging and tearing at his legs and arm as he screamed and stumbled across the covered patio between the cabana and the house. Jamie brought him down in front of Allie and Trevor on the other side of the sliding glass door, his screams incoherent, he was on his back, covering his head with his arms, trying to fend Jamie off with his feet.

He rolled to one side and made another desperate dash for the woods. Jamie caught him again, this time on the lawn, tearing at his legs, ripping his filthy jeans. The suspect howled like a wounded animal as he tried to get to the trail. Jamie took him down on the grass as a wolf takes down a fleeing deer. The invader's inhuman, guttural screams sounded as if blood was gurgling in his throat.

The second Hitchcock turned his head to the cacophony of screams and growls, the Asian suspect twisted and slammed his right shin bone into

Hitchcock's left hip socket. Searing pain shot from his hip down his leg, causing him to wobble.

Ignoring the pain, Hitchcock feinted a left jab. When the Asian began the blocking move he expected, he shifted his weight into a right cross, smashing the suspect's mouth with a thud, knocking him backward. The back of his head smacked the brick wall so hard he slid down the wall to the concrete, out cold.

"Help! Call him off me! Call him off me!" The white suspect begged as he laid in a fetal position on the lawn. Hitchcock ran to Jamie's side.

He took Jamie's collar in hand. "Jamie—Out!" The dog stepped back, snarling. "Lay still. Don't move and you'll be safe."

"I-I'm bleeding!" He shrieked between gasps, his voice grating like a metal file. Hitchcock looked him over. His pant legs and shirt sleeve were shredded, the flesh of his left arm and leg were torn and bloody.

"You're not gonna die. You're under arrest for Attempted First Degree Burglary. Shut up unless I tell you to talk. We'll call an ambulance to check you out. Stay where you are. Jamie..." Hitchcock pointed to the white intruder, curled into a fetal position. "Watch 'em!"

Jamie stood three feet away, growling through bared teeth at the trembling, whimpering criminal.

Allie slid the glass door open, Trevor clinging to her knee. "The station called back. They're on their way," she yelled in a stressed voice.

"Call an ambulance too. They're gonna need it."

He strode back to the carport and stood over the Asian intruder lying stone-still on the concrete floor. He was bleeding from the mouth. "Get up. You and your partner are under arrest for Attempted First Degree Burglary and Assaulting a Police Officer."

No response. He stared at his assailant, noting that the sense of warning that hung over him for two days was gone.

Allie came up alongside him and linked her arm under his. Staring at the fallen attacker, she leaned her head against his arm. "Thank God we're safe now, honey," she said softly, her body shaking.

Hitchcock didn't move or take his eyes off the human panther at his feet. From his experiences in Southeast Asia, he knew this enemy could be faking.

"Wait for me inside, baby. Take care of Trevor. I want to be here when the troops arrive," he told her, his voice a notch above a whisper.

Allie left. Police sirens filled the air and Hitchcock gave the suspect's side a hard nudge with his foot...

ACKNOWLEDGEMENTS

The successful bringing to life of the events, characters and settings in *Day Shift* was the result of the contributions of former Bellevue Police Officers Robert Littlejohn, Jim Massinger, Craig Turi, Bob Phelan, Larry Halvorson, and former officers of the Seattle Police Department. The pencil sketch of the Pancake Corral is the work of my longtime friend and high school classmate, Ira Mandas. I wish also to thank the heirs and current owners of the historic Pancake Corral, who appear often in this series, Ada Williams and Jane Zakskorn for allowing me to have many book signings at the Corral.

ABOUT THE AUTHOR

JOHN HANSEN draws from personal experience for most of his writing. Between 1966-1970 he served as a Gunners Mate aboard an amphibious assault ship that ran solo missions in and out of the rivers and waterways of South Vietnam and other places.

While a patrol officer with the Bellevue Police Department, his fellow officers nicknamed him "Mad Dog" for his tenacity. After ten years in Patrol, he served eleven years as a detective, investigating homicide, suicide, robbery, assault, arson and rape cases.

As a private investigator since retirement, his cases have taken him across the United States and to other countries and continents. He is the winner of several awards for his books, short stories and essays.

Made in the USA
Middletown, DE
28 October 2021